RISE OF THE VENARI
RHAPTAVERSE CHRONICLES BOOK 1

LILY SKYY

Rise of the Venari

First Edition: November 2023

ISBN 978-1-959039-82-2 (ebook)
ISBN 978-1-959039-83-9 (paperback)

Published by Books to Hook Publishing, LLC.
www.BooksToHook.com

CONTENTS

CHAPTER I

PREPARATIONS

"One-hundred ninety-eight. One-hundred ninety-nine. Two hundred."

Kareem blew out a shaky breath as he pushed through his last press-up, sweat dripping down his head. It was barely half-past six in the morning, and he had already completed his daily exercises, going through the same routine he had done for the last few years.

Sitting up in a kneeling position, he closed his eyes and prepared himself for his morning meditation, the next step in his routine. He tried to focus on the day ahead of him but kept getting distracted by how nice the breeze felt as it rushed through the trees and over his sweaty skin. The sound of the stream bubbled nearby, tempting him, but he needed to finish his routine. Today was one of the biggest days in his life, and he couldn't slip up now. He had been waiting for this for years.

Above him, the unwavering African sun was slowly making its way into the sky, reminding him that he had a little over an hour before he had to be at the house of the venari. Closing his eyes again, he focused on grounding himself, steadying his Aura, and mentally planning out his day.

Up early, are we? came a voice in his mind.

Kareem's eyes snapped open to see his older brother Tejas stepping lightly through the trees toward him. Not a single branch or errant twig clung to his dark clothes like they did to Kareem's every time he came out here. He was also lithe compared to Kareem's stockiness; it was hard to believe that Tejas was twelve years his elder.

You know what today is, Kareem replied back into his mind, an ability all Anunnaki had with each other; the ability to communicate through thought. *Today of all days, I can't slip up. I need to be ready.* He closed his eyes again as Tejas sat opposite him with a faint smile on his face.

You? Slip up? I know seasoned warriors who don't have the discipline you do. If Commander Kartik knew a thirteen-year-old boy had more dedication than some of his best men, you would be heading to the warrior's quarter this morning instead of the house of the venari, Tejas said.

Kareem peeked an eye open, catching sight of the city wall far behind him, past the field beyond the edge of the tree line. Even this far out, he could just barely make out the patrols on the wall by the red clothing and paint that adorned the skin of all the warriors. He snorted and closed his eyes again.

The demand for venari is much higher, Kareem said with hands resting on his knees. *And how can you say that? You're a venari yourself.*

Ah, yes, but I never had a choice. Not like you do, Tejas replied. Kareem opened his eyes again and found his brother leaning back, absently picking at blades of long grass. Up until a few years ago, being venari was practically a shunned occupation, and only the unluckiest of the Anunnaki were tapped to join them—which was ironic because Tejas's ability was luck. He had been selected at a young age to join the house of venari and had dedicated his life to hunting down ubir around the world.

With the new queen and all of the changes that had taken place in the great city of Rhapta, being venari had become one of the most coveted positions in the last five years. Not only were the venari under the good eye of the queen, but the job was also dangerous and mysterious, earning someone great admiration and pride from the public. Kareem remembered when he was little; people used to look at Tejas and the dark clothing like he was a ghost or a bad omen, even when Kareem and their family had nothing but the greatest respect for him. Yet now, people smiled at him in the streets, and children begged to hear tales of the human cities and their technology, something few Rhaptans got to see.

Kareem set his brows and said, *Well, my choice is to become a great venari. Mamma and Father think it is a brave choice, and I want to set a good example for Akilah.*

Tejas huffed a laugh. *Akilah is barely seven, and her ability hasn't presented itself yet. She has years before she decides. Look, I'm not trying to dissuade you. The venari are needed, and even though the training is brutal, I know you of all people are the most prepared. I just want to make sure you are confident this is what you want. People think all we do is travel the world and collect stories to tell, but Kareem, what we have to do is... hard. Really hard.*

Kareem slid a leg out and leaned sideways, stretching the aching muscles. *I know that, you've told me a million times. This is the right thing to do, though. The ubir are still running rampant and need to be taken care of. Besides, my ability isn't needed elsewhere.* He tried not to scowl.

Kareem remembered how disappointed he had been when, at eleven years old, his ability had presented itself to him like a forgotten birthday present. He had set a cup down on the table, and it had stuck like the strongest of glues. He had pried and pulled at the cup when, a few minutes later, it had unceremoniously come unstuck and splashed the contents all over his face. Akilah had watched the whole thing, bursting out into laughter at the liquid dribbling onto his clothes. Making things temporarily stick together was not exactly an ability coveted by the venari, but they would take anything these days, and Kareem wasn't about to let pride get the better of him.

Well, I'm not going to hold you back, Tejas said, leaning forward to clap a hand on his shoulder. *From what I've seen, things are different now... better. You even get to work in teams instead of alone.*

Kareem nodded, already having gathered every scrap of knowledge about the venari training as he could. Training typically started at fifteen, but over the years, the venari had changed their ways and allowed younger recruits, giving them several years to train before letting them out on their own. Kareem had heard of a few people at his school who had claimed they were going to join this year; he wondered if he would see any of them or not. There were thousands of children in the city, and the house had to start limiting the number of pupils that took in. Kareem knew the only reason they allowed him and his lackluster ability in was because of Tejas. Still, he wouldn't let that dampen his eagerness. You didn't need legendary abilities to be a good venari, and he intended to be the best.

Kareem stretched out the other leg and started on that side, leaning as far down as he could until the muscle felt like it was at its limit. The breeze had switched directions and was now coming from the direction of the city, bringing with it the smell of bakeries and the sound of early morning in Rhapta. Somewhere in the huge city were other pupils just waking and getting ready for the day. Were they in as much anticipation as he was? What would his team be like? How soon would they go out on their first assignments?

He glanced over at his older brother, who had been like a third parent most of his life. *How long until you have to leave again?* Kareem asked, changing the subject.

A few weeks, I think, Tejas replied. *It'll go by fast, though, and before I know it, I'll be lying on a beach in Bali.* He leaned back in the grass, putting his hands behind his head and looking up at the trees. Kareem grinned at his brother's joke. It was true the life of a venari was hard, and no walk on the beach.

What will you do with all of your free time until then? Kareem asked, getting to his feet and stripping down to the loose shorts he wore. He picked his way through the grass toward the stream.

This and that, Tejas replied. *Ah, that reminds me of why I came out here. I wanted to see if you wanted to get something to eat before you go to the house.* He had closed his eyes and looked serene in the shade.

Sure, Kareem replied, plunging into the water. It was cool and refreshing as he ducked his head under. A thought had him smiling when he came up and spotted Tejas in the same spot. Kareem took a handful of water and chucked it toward his brother.

Kareem's smile wilted when he saw the droplets land everywhere *except* on the now-laughing Tejas. He huffed in annoyance and went back to washing himself in the stream.

You should know better by now, little brother, Tejas said, getting to his feet. *And hurry up; I want to see if there are any steamed lemon buns left.*

Kareem scrubbed faster, intending not to be left behind.

DESPITE BEING thousands of years old, the city of Rhapta was built on clean lines and straight boulevards that bisected the many plazas. The white limestone buildings were long and flat-topped and did an excellent job of keeping out the heat that was already beating down this morning. Kareem had seen pictures of human cities, and he was proud of how organized and structured Rhapta was by comparison. It was sectioned into the north, south, east, and west quarters with the central plaza in the center. Two wide boulevards cut through the entire city, going perpendicular to each other, each lined with small varieties of baobab trees. It was orderly and magnificent at the same time, unlike the cacophonous crowd that had gathered outside one of the food stalls in the central plaza.

Kareem pursed his lips at the chaos of early morning workers trying to get their breakfast before heading to work. *Tejas, I think you are out of luck for once. There isn't going to be anything left,* he said, looking at the group of people gathered in front of the stall they had decided on. Just then, the stall owner shouted that he was sold out and to come back tomorrow. The group moaned and started to disperse, but Tejas patiently waited for them to leave.

Let's just double-check, Tejas said innocently, hands clasped behind his back.

He just said he's sold out, Kareem said, pointing to the stall owner. *Let's go find something else.*

Just a moment, Kareem, Tejas said, heading up to the owner. *Sir, do you happen to have any steamed lemon buns left?*

The owner gave him a droll look. *I just said I was out, kid.* Tejas was short-statured like Kareem, and it was always funny when people assumed he was much younger than he actually was.

If you could double-check, I would be grateful. Tejas waited patiently.

The owner sighed and turned around, rifling through the cloth-lined baskets at the back of the stall. *Ah—oh!* the owner said, coming back to the front, holding a large white bun. *It looks like I missed one. Lemon, too.*

Tejas thanked the man and paid for the bun before turning

back to Kareem with a know-it-all smile. *Looks like my luck is doing just fine,* he said, ripping the bun in half and handing it to Kareem.

Kareem just rolled his eyes and took the piece, lemon custard spilling over onto his fingers. It was hot, and he quickly licked it up, enjoying the tart sweetness. Anunnaki didn't need to eat as much as humans, but that didn't stop it from being enjoyable. Tejas liked to indulge much more than Kareem did, but he wasn't going to turn down the offer from his brother.

They wandered around the central plaza until they came to rest on the lip of a long, shallow pool to watch the people coming and going. The plaza itself was huge, with the behemoth that was the Grand Hall sitting on the north side. The remaining three sides were crowded with buildings of business, the library, and swaths of food stalls that came and went each day. The indigo-robed scholars were the most numerous of those rushing at this time of day, carrying books and scrolls with short, quick steps to the library. Kareem also saw a few white-robed Elders speaking with one of the queen's advisers. The adviser's black robes were a stark contrast to the limestone of the buildings, making them stand out like beacons. The only other person dressed so darkly was Tejas, always in his venari clothing. Soon, Kareem would be dressed the same.

Tejas glanced up at the sun. *It's almost time. Do you need help gathering your things?*

Kareem shook his head. *No, I want to do it myself. I have every-thing packed anyway. I just need to say goodbye to Mamma, Father, and Akilah.*

All right, Tejas said with a proud smile, *I've got a few things to do today, but I'll probably see you around the house. Good luck, Kareem.* He rubbed a hand over Kareem's short hair and headed off toward the west side of the plaza.

Kareem took a steadying breath. He had wanted things for

years and had been preparing for almost as long. He knew every-thing there was to know about the venari and trained himself physically and mentally daily. The next step was just to arrive.

He could do this.

CHAPTER 2
THE HOUSE OF THE VENARI

The side streets just off the east side of the central plaza were much quieter, with only a few people coming and going. The buildings on this street were long and low, only two stories at most. Kareem already knew the house of the venari was the one without windows. A set of large, wooden double doors stood forebodingly at the front with no sign or indication that the city's venari lived and trained here. Kareem eagerly hiked his bag further up his shoulder and knocked three times. He thought he could hear the faint sound of people training coming from the roof, but he couldn't be sure.

The door opened quickly to reveal a bored man with arms as thick as an ox. Before he had a chance to say anything, Kareem interjected.

Hello, my name is Kareem Maamoum. I'm one of the new venari pupils, and I'm to start training today. I'm supposed to arrive by half-past seven, and here I am. He adjusted the strap digging into his shoulder.

The big man raised an eyebrow. *Well, Kareem Maamoum, new*

venari pupil, you might as well come in. He moved to the side, allowing Kareem to see into the darkness beyond.

Kareem nodded his thanks and stepped inside, immediately getting a whiff of sweat and... mint? As he moved inside, he quickly discovered what he had heard were the sounds of training, but they weren't coming from the roof. There was a short dark hallway that opened up to the center of the building where daylight illuminated the center space like they were at the bottom of a deep well. In the middle sat a massive open-air training ring filled with sand, sunlight, and fresh air coming in from above. Inside were many pupils and full-fledged venari locked in combat of various styles. Kareem looked around in wonder. He had heard about the house of the venari many times but was never allowed inside.

There were two levels, both open to the training ring, with many doors on each floor. Kareem could see dark hallways extending off between a few doors, leading deeper into the north and south wings of the building. Despite the outside of the building being built with the white limestone as the rest of the city, the interior of the house was lined with dark wood floors, railings, and staircases along the hallways. The venari themselves wore the same dark human clothing as Tejas, almost utilitarian in style. The pupils, however, had on gray training uniforms. Loose clothing that tightened around shins and forearms made it harder for the fabric to get in the way and slip around during combat while still giving the wearer flexibility. Within the groups fighting in the ring, the dark-clothed venari were clearly the better fighters, their movements precise and quick compared to their bumbling, gray-clothed counterparts.

From where he stood, Kareem could see a few other pupils that wore neither the dark nor gray clothing of the venari or pupils. He knew there were nearly twenty new recruits this year that were all moving in today as well. Some of them lounged confidently against the railing on the upper floor, watching the activities in the ring, while others stayed in the shadow, hurrying to find where they needed to be.

Your room is this way, young one, the big man said, indicating a narrow wooden staircase to the left. He began telling Kareem about the house as he marched up the stairs, Kareem right behind him. *Boys' rooms are in the north wing, and girls' rooms are in the south. You saw the main training ring in the center, and most of the rooms surrounding it are offices or classrooms. You'll receive your schedule later this evening after Savar's introductions. While you are here, you will give respect to the venari; if they tell you to do something, you do it. Other than that, there are not many rules. Savar believes in natural consequences as much as possible unless you put someone else in danger. With that being said, there are no restrictions on using your ability, but be warned, if you harm another unjustly, the consequences are extensive.*

Kareem had to restrain himself from mentioning that he didn't need that speech. It's not like he could stick someone to a chair to death. His ability wore off within minutes. *Yes, sir,* he said anyway. They had followed the upper walkway halfway around the training ring before turning left down one of the dark halls that led deeper into the north wing, where he got another whiff of the mint scent. In here, blue Aurastones sat at intervals along the walls to light the way. Aurastones—their true name was Magalkan'a—were revered all over the city, and it was believed that the Anunnaki's abilities came from the large deposit that Rhapta sat on for the last several thousand years. They were a comforting presence all around the city, always emitting a faint blue light.

They passed several doors without stopping, taking a few turns here and there. Kareem hoped he would remember how to find his room in the maze of dim hallways. They eventually came to an area where mostly gray-clad pupils wandered about, and the big man stopped before an open door on the right.

Here is your room. I'm not sure where your roommate has gone off to, but you'll meet him soon, he said. *Savar will be giving a speech in—*

In fifteen minutes, Kareem said, stepping inside. *I know. I read the letter that was sent to me with the first day's instructions. I'm sure I can find my way back.*

The big man exhaled. *All right then, good luck, and don't die.* He went back the way they came.

Kareem wondered how likely it was that he would really die, especially during training. The thought was quickly replaced by his inspection of the room. It was small at best, with four walls, no windows, and plain furniture. There were two beds, two desks, and two shelves for clothing. One side of the room was already filled with bedding, clothing, and a few small bags. The shelf had a stack of books and scrolls as well. Kareem nodded in approval. Pupils were told to bring minimal items since they wouldn't need much during training. The life of the venari was not one of luxury, and material items were mostly related to their needs on an assignment.

Placing his single bag on the empty bed relieved the building tension in his shoulder. He had brought nothing but the bare necessities. He did have a few beloved books and knickknacks, but he left those with his parents. They didn't mind keeping his extra things in case he wanted them in the future. His mother had been a tearful mess when he had gone to say goodbye. It wasn't a true goodbye, though; he was just living on the other side of the city. Even Akilah had understood he wasn't really going away, only starting a new chapter in his life.

As he was untying his bag, he heard a sound at the door. He turned to find a kid roughly the same age as Kareem standing there with a scrunched expression. He was looking around at Kareem as the bag he had placed on the bed and in his hands was a large book.

Kareem brightened. *Hello, you must be my roommate,* he said as the boy walked into the room without greeting.

Yes, hello, I'm Ovi, the boy said, heading over to his bookshelf, no longer making eye contact.

Well, it's nice to meet you, Kareem said, holding out his hand.

The boy flinched back away from him. *I don't like to be touched. Sorry,* he said, turning back to his bookshelf to place the large volume next to the others. He didn't say anything else, so Kareem dropped his hand. Maybe he was shy?

Not wanting to bother him, Kareem went back to his bag while Ovi went through his own items. It wouldn't take long for Kareem to unpack, and he still had a few minutes before he needed to head to the training ring anyway. He was itching to see the rest of the large building and didn't want to get lost in the future.

Hey, he said, turning around, *do you want to go look around a bit? Maybe get the lay of the land?*

Ovi turned to look at him over his shoulder from his hunched position on the floor. *No way. Savar's speech is in ten minutes. I can't be late,* he said, looking almost annoyed that Kareem had asked. He turned back around without waiting for an answer.

Kareem internally sighed but only shrugged his shoulders. He might need to work on getting his roommate to open up a bit. In the meantime, he wanted to get a head start on anything he could, so he left his half-unpacked bag on the bed and headed out into the hall.

He initially turned right but quickly got turned around and had to head back left. All of the doors were identical as he walked this section of the north wing. After a minute of wandering, he realized the halls were set up in a cloverleaf design with several dead ends and only a few halls that actually led back out. He only discovered this by following the trail of people coming in and out. He nodded and said hello to those in passing, noting the different abilities he saw. Many had the flashy elemental abilities of wind or water, while others' skin and features shifted at will. Kareem knew that many abilities were not seen by the eye, much like his own, but it was still interesting to watch the conspicuous ones. As he got closer to venari rooms, he saw a black-clad man stride past him trailing mist behind. As he turned the corner, the mist flicked around the corner with him like a cat scampering after its master.

It didn't take long to get back to the main walkway that looked down over the training ring. There were a few people gathered there, but it didn't look like anything was starting yet, so Kareem kept going toward the south wing. As he passed the rooms by the training ring, he peeked in, spotting worn desks and chairs, books, and scrolls, and a few older venari setting up. *These must be some of the classrooms,* Kareem thought as he moved on to another hallway leading deeper to the south wing.

This side of the building looked much like the other half. A cloverleaf design of rooms with identical doors. Some were open, others closed, and everything was just as sparse with the lingering scent of mint. As he turned to head back, he saw a group of girls standing off to the side. One of them was holding her hands out, palms up for the others to see. Kareem thought he saw the air practically ripple in waves above her hands. He didn't know what it was supposed to do, but the others hummed in appreciation, smiling at the girl.

Kareem was so absorbed in watching the ripples that he suddenly found himself colliding with a wall of bags hard enough to knock both him and the unsuspecting bags to the ground. It took him a moment to realize what had happened before he struggled to sit up. He was unharmed but a little confused. The group of girls shrieked with laughter as he got to his feet, and he realized it wasn't a wall of bags but a man carrying way too many at once. He looked terrified as he quickly set to pick them all up.

I am so sorry— Kareem started to say as he reached for the bags.

You should be! came a shrill voice in his head. *Is there something wrong with your eyes?* The voice came from a girl standing behind the man. She was slightly taller than Kareem with scornful eyes as she looked down at him. Her waist-length hair was set into many shiny twists that she swung behind her shoulder. His immediate thought was how impractical they were for a venari.

I said I was sorry, he stated hotly. *Is this your father?*

The girl gave a faint scoff. *This is our serving man,* she said. *I pay him good money to carry my bags safely. And now you've kept him from doing his job.*

Zara, one of the girls from the group to the side, called. Her hair was shorn almost to her scalp. *Leave the poor boy alone. His family obviously has never had a serving man before.* The group giggled as they looked Kareem over.

Zara stood in front of him imperiously as if he was the one blocking her path and not the other way around. The man had gathered nearly all the bags into his arms again and set off down the hall.

That's no excuse, Zara said. *Those bags are expensive.* Kareem was annoyed when she gave him a sardonic smile, the full apples of her cheeks rising under her eyes.

Are all of those really necessary? Kareem asked, watching the man struggle down the hall, teetering under the weight. *We were only supposed to bring the basic necessities.* He assumed it was her first day as well since she was dressed in neither venari darks nor pupil grays.

Who are you to tell me what is necessary? she said, her voice like ice. Kareem could have sworn the hall actually cooled just then.

If you want to be a good venari—

Then I wouldn't be asking you for advice. She gave him one last look like she was inviting him to say something and then brushed past him down the hall. Kareem turned to watch her go, incredulous at her rudeness. Shaking his head, he went back the way he was heading, the group of girls giggling again as he went by.

As he got close to the main walkway again, he realized the new pupils were now filing down to the training grounds, with many of the venari lingering on the upper floor around the railing. Putting the rude girl out of his mind, Kareem hurried down the staircase to the sand below, finding himself a spot in the middle. Thankfully, nothing had started yet.

The group was facing toward the back of the ring, and he could see why. Standing up front were several men and a few women, most of which were now household names among the Anunnaki. The oldest man stood in the middle. Tall and wiry, Savar Basu had been the leader of the venari for decades, though he hardly looked like he was in his sixties. He stood with a ramrod-straight posture, surveying the new pupils that were filing in. To his right stood the only other man more well-known than Savar. Zaid Hatem was known in every city circle, not just for being Savar's apprentice and future head of the venari. He was also the queen's consort. Kareem spotted a few girls in front of him trying shamefully to make eye contact with Zaid, who looked almost as austere as Savar. The last person of note was behind Savar to his left. A muscular woman stood with arms crossed while two other venari leaned against the railing behind her. A dark hood hid her features in shadows, but Kareem knew it was Hessa Darvish. She was a few years younger than Tejas but had risen among the venari quickly by bringing in nearly double the ubir that most venari did, and without a scratch on her. Kareem remembered a few of his classmates claiming that she was a literal goddess. Even among the venari, she was spoken of in awe.

Thank you all for assembling so quickly today, Savar started abruptly. His voice was quiet but firm in the minds of the pupils, commanding them to be silent. The crowd quieted down, and Kareem turned to see Zara just now entering the ring with two other girls beside her. They settled in at the back of the group.

My name is Savar, and many of you will know me as the long-

standing head of the venari. You will get to know the other trainers and me very well in the coming months and hopefully years, he continued. *You've all been given short instructions on what today entails, but I will now divulge what will happen going forward. You've all either been tapped or have chosen of your own free will to join the venari ranks. In the past five years, our number has tripled due to some sort of popularity.* Savar glanced briefly at Zaid before continuing. *We've updated our approach to training, but it will be difficult, to say the least. If you think you will come out of training unscathed, this is your chance to leave.*

He paused, waiting to see if any pupils took him up on the offer.

You all know the sole purpose of the venari is to hunt down, capture, and return the ubir to Rhapta. The venari are truly humanity's first protectors against the ubir, and by extension, our first protectors against humanity. The life of a venari is harsh and unforgiving. Your life will be devoted to the cause, and you may be away from the city and your families for long periods of time. What you have to do on those assignments will be even harder. The ubir were all Anunnaki once. Mothers, cousins, and brothers, all of whom have gone mad and now practice the blood rite. Remember that. When you are out there hunting down ubir, you are bringing back someone's family to be executed.

The room had gone deadly quiet. Savar's words weren't unknown, but hearing them was sobering.

As far as your training, he continued, *it may take several years before you are allowed to graduate to a full venari. You will each have a partner for the duration of your training and potentially your life as venari. You've already met them; your roommates will be your partners.*

Kareem internally sighed.

In addition, throughout training, you will be placed in teams of four, and each team will have a venari mentor. There will be trials to complete as a team as well as in pairs. The venari rarely work alone now, so learning to work as a group cohesively will be your primary focus. You need to rely on each other's strengths and balance out your weaknesses.

When you are out in the world, you will only have each other. If one of you falls, you all fall. I expect that some of you will not even make it through training. You will graduate into full venari when you complete three unsupervised assignments and you have your mentor's approval that you are ready. Some of you will be ready sooner than others, but you will not graduate until your entire team is ready. So, focus on building each other up instead of only yourselves.

Excitement was building in Kareem, making his fingers drum on his pant leg. He intended to graduate in record time, so his team had better be ready. He shuffled from foot to foot, eager to begin.

Savar took a breath, glancing around the room. *Now, we'll sort you into groups and assign mentors. We will have a preliminary exam shortly. After that, you are free for lunch, and then the classes begin in the afternoon. The real work begins tomorrow, though.* He turned and nodded to Zaid, who pulled out a piece of paper and stepped forward.

An exam? Kareem thought. He hadn't heard about an exam on the first day. He hadn't prepared for that at all. What could they be testing them on? Venari history?

The following pairs will become teams, Zaid called, reading from the list in a deep voice. *Caden El Tain and Idris Lajami will be paired with Faiza Shahd and Inaam Kirdar.*

Kareem heard a few boys groan.

Zaid went down the list. There was a total of five teams, with one team being short a person. Apparently, "fair" was not a term known within the venari. Finally, Kareem heard his own name called.

Kareem Maamoum and Ovi Fadel will be paired with… Zara al-Hazmi and Benita Chudasama.

Kareem wanted to scream. The chances of there being more than one Zara were slim. He turned around, and sure enough, Zara was glaring daggers down her haughty nose. Exhaling hard, he turned back to the front.

Zaid had folded up his paper. *If everyone could find their teams and get together, your mentor will be with you in a moment. They will give you more details on what is to come next and what will be expected of you in the coming months.*

The group moved, people coming together to find their teammates. Kareem had started the day feeling so confident and prepared. Could he really not graduate until the entire team was deemed worthy? There had to be some way out of this. Zara looked like she would be one of the first to drop out, and Ovi wasn't a good sign so far.

Focus, Kareem! he berated himself. There was no way he was going to do this with that sort of attitude. There had to be some way through this. Even if his teammates failed to do their part, the trainers would have to see he was fit enough to be venari. He would make sure of it.

Unclenching his fists, he went to find his team.

CHAPTER 3

THE EXAM

Looking around the room, Kareem spotted Ovi first trudging toward him. They both heard quick footsteps stalking toward them in the sand and found Zara making her way over.

I'm guessing this is Ovi, she said, looking over Kareem's partner like he didn't impress her.

Yeah, Ovi, this is Zara, Kareem said reluctantly. *Where is your roommate?*

How am I supposed to know? she replied, crossing her arms. Just then, a smaller girl with short, dense curls sidled up to them.

Hi, I'm Binita, she said with a small wave. Zara frowned at her while Kareem and Ovi said their hellos. They stood there in silence at the edge of the ring, waiting for their mentor. Zara kept tossing her hair over her shoulder and stepping away from the group to glance toward the front, where Zaid stood talking to Savar. Binita rolled her eyes, and Kareem was inclined to agree. Was Zara batting her eyelashes?!

The other teams had gathered similarly while older pupils and venari hung around the railing as if waiting for something. They were pointing and grinning at a few of the new recruits. Soon, a young man came up to their group wearing the venari darks.

He had a friendly smile on his face. *Hello,* he said with a nod. *I am Neelan Qureshi. I'll be your mentor for the duration of your training. I assume you all are,* he looked down at a piece of paper, *Kareem, Ovi, Zara, and Binita?*

Yes, that's us, Kareem said while the others nodded their heads. Kareem had never seen this venari before, but that wasn't unusual. Most of them were out on assignments or training other pupils and didn't spend much time wandering around the city. He looked roughly Tejas's age with an open face and unusual green eyes. This was uncommon compared to the usual brown or black eyes of the Anunnaki, and they stood out against his dark skin.

Good! Neelan said, rolling up the piece of paper. *Then we might as well get started. I'd just like to say welcome. I know choosing to become venari, or having it chosen for you, is a hard thing, but I think we can make you all into fine venari one day. As Savar mentioned, I will be with you for your entire training years, and ultimately you will need my approval to graduate. But we'll have more time later to get to know one another.*

There's going to be an exam? Kareem cut in. More venari and pupils had gathered at the railings, and he was starting to get nervous. Would they be performing a skill?

Yes, Neelan said, clasping his hands together and looking at each of them. *In about half an hour, you and the other new pupils will have a skirmish, but I'll explain the details in a few minutes. We have a few housekeeping items to go over.*

A skirmish? But they hadn't even learned anything yet! Were they going to be graded on this skirmish? He should have done more stretches this morning.

As I was saying, you'll need to prove to me that you are capable of being venari. Over the course of your training, you will have skirmishes against other teams every three months. These skirmishes are meant to show both Savar and me your skills and how you are progressing as a team. If at any time Savar or I believe that you are not cut out to be venari, we will notify you, and you will be expected to leave immediately. You will not get to try again in the future.

Kareem's heart was pounding at the prospect of getting kicked out. *Why would that happen? Don't we need more venari?*

Neelan dipped his chin in agreement. *Yes, but we are not so desperate that we are willing to put others in danger if you are unable to do your job. Remember, you are working in teams and pairs for the rest of your life. In addition, there are very strict rules that the Anunnaki have to follow when we go out into the human world. We can't risk you putting all of us in danger if you are unable to follow the rules. Humans cannot know of us.*

The others were looking as grim as Kareem felt.

The path to graduation from your venari training is to complete three unsupervised assignments successfully, Neelan continued, crossing his arms. *You are allowed to go on an unsupervised assignment when you have completed one supervised assignment—with me— and have won a skirmish.*

So, winning the skirmishes isn't just about proving to you that we aren't failing miserably, Zara said.

That's right, Neelan said. *You need to win skirmishes to be able to go on unsupervised assignments. And you need unsupervised assignments to graduate. The first skirmish today does not count, though. It is only used as a preliminary exam for us to decide who your team leader will be and to show us what you can do. A baseline, if you will.*

Great, Ovi said, balling his hands in his sleeves. He looked like he wanted to be anywhere else.

Neelan smiled. *Don't worry, you'll do fine. After this, you are free for a midday break, and then in the afternoon, you will all meet with Hessa Darvish, who is our combat trainer. She'll also go over your schedules and whatnot. For now, we only have a little time left for you to show each other your abilities and formulate a plan of attack. The goal of this skirmish is simple. There will be an Aurastone placed in the center of the ring, and an hourglass will begin. When the last grain of sand falls, whichever team is holding the Aurastone wins.*

That seems simple enough, Kareem said. As long as he could get to the Aurastone and hang onto it, then his team would win. Easy. If he could just get his team to back him up, then they might actually make it. Though, glancing at Binita, who was more focused on looking around the room, he wondered if that was going to be possible.

All right, Kareem said, *I can go first. My ability is pretty straightforward. I can make things stick for a few minutes.*

What? Neelan said, eyebrows knitting together.

Kareem bent down and grabbed a handful of sand, walked over to a nearby post, and pressed it into the wood. The clump of sand hung there while he walked back.

Well, that's... useful, Binita said.

Zara burst out laughing. *That's your ability? What are we supposed to do with that?*

I was thinking I could hang on to the Aurastone pretty easily as long as you all distract the others, Kareem said, squaring his shoulders.

Were you? Zara mocked.

Okay, you must have a better plan. What were you planning to do? Kareem asked.

I did have a better plan, Zara said, and suddenly Kareem started to feel very hot. It happened so quickly he looked up to make sure the sun wasn't right above him. Sweat broke out on his neck and back, and by the looks of the others in their group, he wasn't the only one. The other people in the training ring didn't react as if the temperature had just risen by twenty degrees, though. *I was going to slow them down.*

Okay, you can return the temperature to normal, Neelan said, wiping a hand over his forehead. The air instantly started to cool back down to the normal level of heat that blanketed Rhapta.

So, you can change the temperature? Kareem snorted, flicking his shirt to get a breeze going. *I don't think that's going to do much, and it'll only slow us down as well. It won't look good to Savar.*

Or Zaid, came a deep, mocking voice from where Binita was standing. The four of them turned to where Binita's small body was, but instead of her face under her head of short curls, it was Zaid's face, sneering at Zara. *You wanted to impress him, right?* came the deep voice again.

Zara narrowed her eyes. *I want us to look good to everyone. And mimicking other people's faces is considered rude, Binita.* The smaller girl chuckled in a deep voice as her face shifted, and they were looking at her own features again.

Okay, that was a little disturbing, Kareem said. *So, you can shapeshift?*

Only my face and my voice, the girl said, more focused on swishing her feet back and forth in the sand now. Her voice was back to normal, at a pitch much higher than Zaid's.

All right... Ovi, show us yours, Kareem said, fingers tapping against his biceps.

No, I'd rather not, Ovi said, shaking his head. *I can just—*

What? Zara said at the same time Kareem said, *Hurry up, just show us.*

I said no, Ovi repeated, balling his fists tighter in his sleeves.

Kareem scowled and was about to retort when Neelan cut in. *It's fine, Ovi. Why don't you explain instead? Not all abilities can be shown.*

Ovi tilted his head in resignation. *I can paralyze someone by touching them, except it's painful for them and can... well, it could stop their heart.*

The rest of them just looked at him openmouthed. He could accidentally kill someone by touching them? Kareem knew there were some abilities that were dangerous, but Ovi looked like he belonged among the scholars instead of here with the venari.

Woah, Binita said. *That's heavy.*

Zara took a healthy step away from Ovi.

Yes, thank you for not showing us that one, Neelan said. He was looking around the room now at the other groups to see how they were doing.

Five minutes! Zaid called to the teams and their mentors. He was moving around the room, drawing lines in the sand near each of the teams. When he finished, he placed an Aurastone about the size of a small melon on the center of the ring. It pulsed faintly with blue light, almost imperceptible in the sunlight coming from above.

Okay, planning time is about up, Neelan said, clapping his hands together.

Kareem's heart rate started to pick up. It wasn't enough time! They hadn't planned anything.

I wish you luck and one more thing, don't leave the ring. If you do, you fail automatically. So, stay inside. Neelan backed away and went to stand on the other side of the railing with the other venari and pupils.

Kareem looked around at the four other teams. Some of them were smiling and cheering, while others looked panicked and confused. He definitely felt closer to the second category.

All right, let's come up with a game plan, Kareem said quickly, ushering the others together. Unfortunately, they were hardly listening. Zara looked at him less than impressed and went back to looking around the room for Zaid, Ovi only shuffled half a step closer, and Binita kept changing her face to Zara's to annoy the other girl.

Hey, focus! Kareem said, snapping his fingers. *We want to win, right?*

Zara sighed heavily, looking back at him. *We clearly aren't going to be winning anything. Also, do you think you're in charge here? We don't have a leader, remember?*

Kareem groaned, running a hand over his hair. *Just don't change the temperature for all of us. And if you three can distract everyone else, I can get the Aurastone,* he said, but no one was listening.

Teams, step up to your starting lines! Zaid called, moving to the back of the ring with Savar and Hessa.

Kareem's veins felt like they were buzzing, and his stomach twisted. He moved up to the line Zaid had drawn with the others, dancing on his feet.

Just stay in the ring, he hissed to the others. The other groups were now lined up around the ring at regular intervals. The small Aurastone sat innocently in the center. Kareem made note of some of the other pupils, trying to decipher who would be a reasonable threat and who wouldn't, but it was hard to tell. His heart was pitter-pattering in his chest, and he clenched and unclenched his fingers.

At the back of the ring, Zaid pulled a large hourglass set in bronze metal out of a bag. It glinted in the daylight as he twisted it so all the sand would go to one side. It felt like forever until he tipped it upside down and set it on the nearest railing.

Begin!

Kareem froze. He couldn't make his muscles move.

But so did everyone else. The room had gotten quiet as all the new pupils stared at each other within the ring, waiting for someone to make the first move. The only movement was the sand draining into the hourglass. It was seeing the sand drain that had Kareem's muscles moving. He was the first to burst away from the line, running full speed toward the Aurastone.

The moment Kareem stepped forward, the stillness of the moment broke. All five teams were suddenly kicking up sand to get to the Aurastone. A boy with heavy brows was moving much faster than Kareem was, and he barely made it to the Aurastone before Kareem touched it with the tip of his fingers, sticking it to him.

A third body came slamming into him from the side, and he

was forced to drop the Aurastone to get air into his lungs. The teams were now shouting at each other, some in panic and others barking orders. Kareem scrambled to his feet and was pretty sure the person who had collided with him like a boulder was a slight girl with shorn hair. Was that the same girl from the hallway?

The Aurastone was in the hands of a boy who had the sand shifting underneath his feet like a mudslide, keeping some of the others away. A second later, a girl launched into the air, soaring much farther than should be possible and snatching the Aurastone before hitting the ground and rolling away.

Kareem got to his feet and looked for his team. He spotted Ovi almost back where the starting line was. What was he doing? Kareem growled in frustration and ran toward the current Aurastone possessor. Off to the right, Zara was chatting—*chatting*—with one of the girls she had come in with earlier. Most pupils were chasing after the girl leaping in the air like a graceful frog. At least Binita was chasing after her in the pack of pupils close behind, but her short legs did little to help her keep up.

Kareem ran to intercept the leaping girl, attempting to time his collision just right. The girl was paying attention to the trail of pupils behind her and not Kareem to her right.

He collided with her, grabbing the Aurastone and staying on his feet as his shoulder slammed into the side of her. He heard her yelp out loud, and he grinned at his victory. Just then, the girl Zara had been talking to slapped her hand down on the sand, and a massive shockwave rocked through the training ring, sending Kareem to the ground... again. The shockwave had rattled the building, and venari and older pupils murmured in appreciation while hanging onto the rails as the sand began to settle down.

Kareem coughed and attempted to get up while gripping the Aurastone with two hands. He was suddenly jerked to the right and heard somebody shout in anger.

He's not letting go! a boy yelled, pulling at the Aurastone in

Kareem's hands. He hadn't released his ability this time, so the Aurastone was effectively glued to his hands. Another boy came up behind him, and with a nod to the first kid, they picked up Kareem by his arms and legs and started running toward the edge of the training pit.

They were going to throw him out! It would mean an automatic fail for his team. Kareem squirmed in their arms, but it was no good. He let go of the Aurastone with a growl, and they dropped him to the sand.

By the time he picked his head up, the Aurastone had changed hands three more times. The leaping girl had it again and was bouncing around the ring with the others behind her. One boy caught her by the ankle, and she screamed along with three others nearby. A quick burst of electricity spattered over the boy's hand and through the nearby sand, sending the few pupils close by to the ground. Many of the venari gasped, and some of the pupils pounded their fists, demanding a disqualification.

Savar stood at the back of the ring, unmoving. "Fair" was not the venari way.

The leaping girl was crying on the ground, not moving to get up, and only one of her teammates came to her side while the rest of the skirmish went on. Kareem saw Binita get knocked to the ground by the same girl that had muscled Kareem down, the girl from the hallway.

Kareem glanced at the hourglass as he got up. It was over three-quarters of the way empty already. Whoever had it would soon be the winner. He started hurtling toward the current holder of the Aurastone, a boy tall enough to be fully grown. When anyone would get close to him, they would gasp and retch, causing them to fall back. It looked like he had waited until the timer was almost out before jumping in. As he ran around the ring, there was a bubble of pupils that attempted to get close, only to find themselves retching.

Kareem ran closer, running by Zara in the process. She looked like she was pretending to participate but was holding much further back than necessary. *Are you going to help!?* he shouted at her. There was no point in attempting to get Ovi in, and Binita was a lost cause.

And do what?! Zara shouted back.

I don't know, something!

Fine! They were both running toward the tall boy with the Aurastone when Zara stopped and inhaled.

The temperature of the room plummeted. Zara looked like she was straining, and everyone else in the room exclaimed at the sudden cold. The boy with Aurastone had hunched in on himself against the cold, but Kareem could already feel the temperature rising again. Zara couldn't hold it for long then.

Kareem took the opportunity to run toward the Aurastone. When he got close, he understood what had been happening. He felt an overwhelming repulsion toward the boy with the stone. Nausea rose in his stomach, and he had to fight not to upend the contents of his stomach. His eyes even started watering as he took another step forward.

Come on, Kareem! he screamed in his own mind. *Push!*

He choked as his stomach attempted to heave, but he managed to put one foot in front of the other, and before he knew it, he had his hands locked around the Aurastone in the boy's grasp. Activating his ability, the boy had a hard time shaking and pulling it away. Another boy slammed into them, taking them all to the ground. Kareem managed to pull the Aurastone away and into his stomach, but more pupils had joined the fight in pulling it from him. Kareem was in a sea of bodies, all trying to pull the stone from him, and he gritted his teeth against their abelites. He hoped the boy with the electricity wasn't coming...

Time! Zaid's voice boomed in their minds.

Some of the venari cheered, and most of the new pupils

groaned. It took a few minutes for the pile of pupils to get off a grinning Kareem. He held the Aurastone up in triumph.

I have it! he said as Zaid walked over.

Thank you, Zaid said, taking the Aurastone from him while Kareem beamed. He had done it! He had won his first skirmish.

The new pupils stood and faced Savar, who had moved forward. *That was... interesting to watch,* Savar said, and many of the venari chuckled. *As a reminder, today's skirmish is not counted toward your requirements for graduation. You will need to win the next one to be able to complete an unsupervised assignment. So, today's winner is,* another venari whispered in Savar's ear, *Tarun Munir and his team!*

The venari and older pupils cheered, turning to slap the tall boy with the repulsion ability on his back as Kareem looked around in confusion.

Please see to your mentors for your next instructions, Savar said, and the venari began to disperse back into the halls.

Kareem looked around in a panic for Neelan. He had been the winner! Not that other guy. What happened? Something wasn't right, and he needed to tell Savar. Kareem spotted Neelan in the corner with Binita and Zara, and Ovi was just coming over.

What happened?! Kareem asked as he ran up to them. *I won!*

Neelan gave him a halfhearted smile. *Your team was disqualified because Binita got tossed out of the ring.*

Kareem turned to Binita, who didn't even have the audacity to look ashamed. She only shrugged. *Not much I could have done about it.*

How is that fair? Kareem exclaimed. *None of them were even help-ing me!*

Calm yourself, Kareem, Neelan said with a touch of annoyance. *This was just a preliminary examination. It doesn't have much weight in the grand scheme of things. Right now, you are free to eat lunch or take a rest. After that, you'll meet with Hessa for the afternoon. Don't worry, I've seen teams do worse,* Neelan said, chuckling now.

So, who is our team leader? Zara asked. She had a know-it-all look on her face, like she had predicted their loss.

You'll find out this evening after your classes, Neelan said. He left them there in the sand and went with some of the other venari and pupils, heading deeper into one of the ground-level halls, presumably to the eating or resting areas.

Kareem took a long, deep breath, trying to settle the anger. Neelan had said it didn't matter that they had lost, so why should he care? If anything, they should be learning from their mistakes and finding ways to correct them for the next skirmish.

Okay, that was terrible. I know, Kareem said. *But we can come up with a better plan next time. There has to be a better way to win.*

Yeah... sure, Ovi said, seeming less than convinced.

I think we are just going to have to hope that we aren't kicked out, Zara said.

We have to do better than that. We need to be a team so we can win, Kareem said hotly. *How about we all spend our break together and figure out how to combat our weaknesses?*

Zara snorted. *Why don't you work on yours first,* she said and walked off.

Kareem turned to find only Ovi remaining. Binita had already left. *We could still—*

Ovi gave him an awkward half-attempt at a smile, but he turned and left Kareem standing in the sand, following the rest of the pupils out.

Kareem tilted his head back in exasperation. It was going to take a lot of work if he had any intention of becoming venari in the near future. He relented and went to see where everyone was going, following the trail of people and the scent of spices.

CHAPTER 4

UNEXPECTED DEVELOPMENTS

Kareem discovered most people congregated in the dining hall, despite not everyone needing to eat. Anunnaki could realistically go three days or so with only a single meal. Kareem had just eaten this morning, so he decided to spend the break looking around. Maybe he could get training tips from older pupils or venari.

The dining hall was set on the south wing's ground floor, not far off from the training ring. Kareem followed pupils and venari like a school of fish down to the long room lit only by Aurastones. It was packed to the max and seemed to burst with people, as if it had outgrown its intended capacity. A sparse kitchen was off to the left, and tables of food were set out. He knew that the venari took turns cooking meals for everyone. It was one of the many chores they were all required to do at some point, along with regular cleanings of the entire building. The venari were a self-sufficient group and rarely needed to interact with the outside population in Rhapta.

Kareem didn't spot any of his teammates, so he wandered around looking for a place to sit. Some people eyed him as he passed by but refused to make room for him. Others looked him over with sneers and a few with curiosity. He could tell who the new recruits were by a lack of uniform.

Hey, Sticky Fingers! Hey, Sticky! a voice shouted from behind him. At the insistence, Kareem turned to find a group of venari seated at a low table near the side wall, looking at him expectantly. They were crammed together tightly, but one of them—presumably the one who had called to him—was waving him over with a grin on his face. He made his way over to the group, pushing his shoulders back.

As he got close, the guy who was waving said, *You're the one who was hanging onto that Aurastone for dear life, right?* The group laughed at that. He looked no older than nineteen and had a smile that looked a fraction too big for his face, but he wore the venari blacks, so Kareem remained polite.

Yes, that was me, he said, setting his jaw.

Ha! That was an excellent tactic, the guy said, looking around at his friends with approval. *We thought you were a goner for a second there at the end. Is that your ability?*

Realizing he didn't mean to make fun of him, Kareem gave a half-smile and held up his hands, wiggling his finger. *Just my hands, and yes, my ability allows me to make things stick—literally.*

A younger boy out of uniform sitting next to the first guy nudged him. *See? I told you, we literally couldn't pry the thing out of his hands without cutting them off!* Kareem recognized the younger boy as one of the new recruits. He was the one who had made the sand turn to mud in the ring.

The first guy nodded with a smile. *Looks like he does have sticky fingers,* he chuckled. Looking back to Kareem, he said, *My name is Waqas, and this one is my younger brother Aryan who I think you've met in passing.* He said the last part with a smirk. *Come sit with us. These boulder heads will make room for you,* he said, indicating his friends that sat across from him. And they did move over eagerly now that Waqas had invited Kareem in.

We watched the whole thing from above, Waqas said as Kareem sat down across from him.

It's our favorite day of the year, a venari girl said. The others chuckled and agreed.

How'd your team do? Waqas asked, spinning a cup of water between his hands on the table. *We couldn't really tell who was with who.*

Horrendous, Kareem muttered. *If there was a last place, we would have had it.*

No, I could have sworn you guys won! Aryan said.

Kareem shook his head. *One of my team members got tossed out of the ring.*

Oh, Aryan said with a pitying look. We were doing pretty well, but only because of Samira. At Kareem's expression, he elaborated. *She was the one jumping around in the air.*

Kareem was almost jealous that he had such an impressive member. *You're lucky,* he said, and Aryan could only agree.

Yeah, some of the new abilities will be interesting to see in the field, the venari sitting next to Kareem said. He spoke around mouthfuls of a creamy soup.

In the field? Kareem said. *You mean...*

Waqas nodded with a grin. *In the real world. It's much different when you're hunting ubir while trying not to be seen by humans. And the stakes are* much *higher.* He looked like he enjoyed the challenge.

Not much to stop them from disappearing, though, another boy mutter further down the table. Kareem had just barely heard it, but a stream of water shot from Waqas' cup and splashed right into the boy's face.

No need to scare the younglings, Waqas admonished.

The other boy was wiping water from his face, looking at his wet shirt in contempt. *It's true, though. Shouldn't they be prepared?*

They have years, Wael, the girl said, waving a spoon at him. *Savar will figure it out before then.*

Kareem was watching the exchange in confusion. *Figure out what? Who is disappearing?*

Waqas gave Wael an annoyed look before turning to Kareem. *It's nothing to worry about, really. You already know that an initial wave of Anunnaki have been allowed to travel outside the city as a sort of tester, right?*

Kareem nodded. The Anunnaki as a whole had been essentially confined to living within the city barrier for the last several thousand years unless they didn't mind losing their abilities and all of their memories. Only the venari had ever been allowed to use the special ink that allowed them to leave temporarily, just long enough to find and capture the ubir and bring them back. But five years ago, a new version of the ink was created that was permanent, allowing the Anunnaki to leave the city for good if they so chose. It was a miracle, to say the least, since the population had been dwindling for centuries. The queen had even talked about potentially opening up the city to the human world again after thousands of years of being hidden. But that was still pretty far off. For now, the first wave of citizens that wanted to test the ink and travel the world had been allowed to do so over the past two years and had been a success so far.

Well, Waqas continued, *we heard a few of them have gone missing. They are supposed to check in regularly to update the city on their whereabouts for research purposes. But a few of them have... fallen off the grid, so to speak.*

Kareem's brows knit together. *What does that mean? They just didn't call when they should have? Maybe they got tired of checking in.*

Waqas and a few others shook their heads. *The queen has a team of advisers with eyes and ears all over the planet. If the missing Anunnaki had just stopped calling, they would still know where they were. But they literally couldn't find them or proof that they even existed. Everyone that was a part of that initial wave was given identification documents, money, and a paper trail so they could merge into human society, but all records of them are gone.*

Goosebumps spread over Kareem's arms. *What happened to them? Why hasn't the queen called the others back in?*

Waqas leaned back, relaxing a little. *It's only been a couple of people, and the only reason we know is that Zaid knows, and the venari need to be aware when we go out. None of the venari have gone missing; it's only the citizens. And I'm sure the queen and Savar are figuring it out.*

The ink stopped working, Wael said. *I know it did. They all lost their memories and became human.*

The girl sitting next to him snorted. *No, it didn't,* she said. *We have the ink, you idiot.* She lifted up a sleeve to show the circular Anunnaki tattoo they were all born with, marking them as one of the tribe. The venari all had additional designs surrounding them with the new ink, allowing them to come and go from the city as they pleased. Older generations of venari had used the temporary ink that would need to be reapplied before every assignment. The new ink was much more convenient.

If anything was wrong with the ink, the girl continued, *it would have happened to us. No, I'm willing to bet they didn't ever want to come back and ran away, not that they needed to,* she said with a shrug.

Just then, the sound of a bell could be heard from deep within the building. It was loud enough that anyone would have been able to hear it. The group all started gathering their things to get up.

That's the five-minute bell, Waqas said to Kareem. *You and Aryan should hurry, don't want to be late for any class with Hessa.* The other venari chuckled, and one of them even shuddered, the mood much lighter than it had been a minute before. Waqas came over and dropped a hand on Kareem's shoulder as he stood. *Don't worry about what Wael said. That's nothing that you kids need to worry about.* Kareem wanted to point out he wasn't that much older than him, and it was a stretch to call him kid, but he just nodded instead.

Thanks for the advice, Kareem said.

Aryan made his way over to him. *Come on, I know where we are headed. I've heard Hessa is a beast if you're late.*

Kareem didn't need to be told twice.

KAREEM AND ARYAN shuffled into the room amid a crowd of other students. Kareem wanted to find a spot up front, but Aryan was pushing him to the back, and it looked like the ones up front were all taken already. He spied Zara already there with the girl with the shockwave—Inaam, was it?

The ground floor of the north wing held many large, windowless classrooms such as this one. Rows of benches faced a bare wall up front where Hessa stood with the other two venari that had flanked her in the ring earlier. Her hood was pulled back to reveal a stern face and angular cheekbones. Tight braids sat in neat rows against her scalp, ending at the nape of her neck. She stood with arms behind her back, left hand gripping her right wrist as she watched the new recruits file in. Thankfully they didn't have the audience of older pupils and venari this time, and the atmosphere felt quieter, less like they were on display.

Kareem didn't see Ovi or Binita right away, even though he would have liked to have his team sit together, so he sat with Aryan and a few of his teammates. He recognized the leaping girl, Samira, and the boy with the heavy brows who almost beat him to the Aurastone at the beginning of the skirmish. They nodded to him crisply as Hessa stepped forward, and the mental chatter of the class quieted down.

Good afternoon, everyone. My name is Hessa Darvish, and I'm the physical combat instructor for all pupils here at the house. Her words were clipped, but her voice was smooth and steady in Kareem's head. Everyone was already paying rapt attention.

Today I will briefly go over what your schedules will look like going forward and give you an idea of what kind of training you will be completing prior to graduation. I will be very clear; you will hate me by the end of the week. I very well may become the bane of your existence, and if you think you won't be seeing me again after graduation, think again. While not as frequent, venari continue training forever to maintain their skills and abilities. If you cannot handle me, you won't be able to handle what you have to do in the field.

Kareem understood why Savar chose her to be the combat trainer: she was just as severe as he was. He could see a few other pupils' eyes widen at her declaration while others' jaws clenched in defiance.

Hessa had paused speaking and began pacing back and forth at the front of the room. *There are nineteen of you now, but I'm willing to bet at least five of you won't make it through training. There's always the few,* she said as if remembering some in particular. The other venari upfront chuckled. Kareem's fingers dug into his palms. He would *not* be one of those. He couldn't even imagine what he would do with his life if it were not to be a venari.

Starting tomorrow morning, Hessa continued, *you will be expected to be in the training ring at dawn. Not walking to the ring at dawn, standing with your feet planted in the sand as the sun comes up. Latecomers will be punished. You will complete the exercises every morning that I set forth for you. This could include basic conditioning, specialized training, duels, and sparring, as well as ability-focused training later on.* She continued to pace as she spoke. *You will receive your one break each day to use as you please, but you are expected to be in your assigned classes each afternoon. Some of these will be with older pupils, others will be with your current year. Your schedules will be in your rooms this evening, along with your uniforms.*

She stopped and faced the room. *As you were told this morning, skirmishes will be held every three months. That means twelve weeks from now, you will face each other in another challenge, and the victorious team will have a chance to complete an unsupervised assignment as long as other requirements have been met. There is much to learn prior to that, so you must be diligent and focused each and every day. We are not the pompous warriors that strut around the city like peacocks. We face danger every single time we leave the barrier. Remember that.*

You will be spending a lot of time with the people in this room over the next few years and potentially for the rest of your life. Get to know one another and learn your strengths and weaknesses. And more than anything, get to know your teams; they are the ones keeping you alive.

I guess I'm dead then, Kareem thought, crossing his arms.

Hessa motioned to the other two venari in the room. *This is Amol Khanna and Laban Dayal,* she said. *They will be a few of your instructors during your time here as well.* Amol leaned against the front wall, moving only to scratch at the scruff around his skin while Laban lounged on a bench against the wall. His slight frame was wound in layers of dark clothing that looked too hot for the current weather, but not a drop of sweat was on him. In fact, it looked like "uncomfortable" was not something he was familiar with. They both nodded and looked around the room with eyes both knowing and amused. It was clear they didn't think much of the new recruits.

Hessa went over a few other details about the house and its rules and expectations. Kareem's mind started to wander. He had a good vantage point of the back of the heads of every new recruit in the room. He recognized most of them from the skirmish, but he intended to understand their weaknesses as well, whether they liked it or not. He refused to be dismissed from the house of the venari. In fact, he was already picturing himself standing where Hess, Amol, and Laban stood now. He imagined himself a seasoned venari though still young, teaching the newest set of recruits about the dangers of the world and the difficulties they might face. He imagined people looking at him the way they looked at Zaid or Hessa. It was glorious.

Before long, Hessa dismissed them for the rest of the afternoon. It was the last bit of free time they would have before they began tomorrow, and Kareem was eager to look at his schedule. He said goodbye to Aryan with a promise to see him tomorrow and headed for his room. He spotted Ovi's head on his way out the door but soon lost him in the gaggle of people. Other older pupils were changing classes at that time, and he found himself in a sea of gray.

Making his way through the maze of hallways back to the upper floors, Kareem was suddenly yanked to the side into a darker hallway. His gasp quickly turned into a choked scoff upon seeing his brother. *Was that necessary?* he asked, rubbing his arm.

Apparently, Tejas said with a shrug as he leaned against the wall. *How'd it go?*

Terrible, Kareem replied, watching the other pupils drain away to their classrooms or bedrooms. *Did you watch the skirmish?*

No, but I heard about it, Tejas said. *You almost won.* His smile was proud, but Kareem felt anything but.

He snorted. *Our team was horrible, and the only reason we even got the Aurastone was because of me. Do you think there is any way I can switch teams?*

Tejas actually laughed. *Not a chance.*

But you never had teams! Kareem protested.

Yes, and I also had to fend for myself for years. His eyes softened. *I would not wish that upon anyone. You should be thankful you have three people that have your back.*

I'm more likely to get a knife in the back, Kareem muttered, thinking of Zara's sneering looks.

You'll be fine, Tejas said. *I actually came to let you know I was leaving.*

What? Kareem said, looking up. *Another assignment? I thought you would have a little longer.*

Tejas looked up and down the hall before he spoke. *Yes, but more venari have been needed lately. There have been a few citizens that went missing recently, and they want some of us to look into it while out on another assignment.* He looked far more concerned than Waqas had earlier.

Yeah, I heard about that, Kareem said. *But I thought it was being handled?*

Tejas looked like he wanted to laugh again. *Yeah, by us.* He sighed. *I'm going with a team, so there shouldn't be any issues. The only people that have gone missing were alone, so I'm not too worried. I just want to let you know I'm headed out in the morning.*

Kareem nodded, understanding. This was not the first time, nor the fiftieth his brother had left on a dangerous assignment. He had been venari for over ten years now, and him going away was nothing new to Kareem. Still, he said, *Be careful. See you soon?*

Tejas nodded and rubbed a hand on top of Kareem's head. *Good luck, and don't get in any fights.* Kareem rolled his eyes as Tejas disappeared around the corner. As if Kareem would get into a fight.

He made his way back to his room, no longer accosted by the sea of gray pupils. After opening his door, he was disappointed to see Ovi was not there. But sitting on Kareem's bed was a neat stack of gray clothing and two pieces of paper. He lifted the clothing up, and sure enough, it was a gray pupil's uniform in his size. The larger of the two pieces of paper turned out to be his schedule, just as Hessa promised. Daily physical training and afternoons filled with strategy and classroom work. After setting that down, he picked up the last piece of paper. It was small and rolled up tightly, and sealed with wax. Rhaptans rarely bothered with such things anymore, but he assumed this would be who his team leader would be.

He thought about the possibility of his team leader being someone else like Ovi or, Creator forbid, Zara. But he steeled himself for the worst and refused to allow them to hold him back. No matter what, he would be the best venari there was.

He carefully lifted the wax and unrolled the scroll. In jagged, script-like print, it read:

Your team leader will be:

Kareem Maamoum

Kareem grinned. He was definitely looking forward to class tomorrow.

CHAPTER 5

TRAINING BEGINS

Kareem thanked himself a thousand times over that he forced himself to complete his daily exercises for the last three years. He then cursed himself for not pushing himself harder as the sweat poured down his face. The other new pupils ran near him, all sullying their new uniforms with sweat as well.

Almost everyone had made it to the training ring this morning, but two stragglers came in just as the sun was coming up. Hessa proved herself both merciless and true to her word. Not only were the two latecomers punished, but the entire group was forced to run around the perimeter of the city, which was several miles at least, seeing as the quarries flanked the south wall, forcing them to run *around* the quarries as well.

Kareem had listened to the angry grumbles the entire run directed at the two pupils who were now trying their hardest to keep up. Kareem was in the middle of the pack, he had a good pace, but he didn't have the mile-long legs of some of the other kids. Binita was actually ahead of him, and he was impressed, to say the least. He didn't see Zara or Ovi, though, meaning they were somewhere behind him.

He had tried to talk to Ovi when he got back later last night, but the other boy hardly said two words to him. He didn't seem angry, only wanting to be left alone. Kareem had wanted to immediately start strategizing how best to get his team into an organized unit, but the moment Zara had shown up in the ring this morning, he knew it was going to be a near-impossible feat. She had arrived with Inaam and the girl with the shorn hair from the hallway, whose name he discovered was Faiza. They came as close as possible to sunrise, and Zara wouldn't even look at him. How did she expect to graduate if she wasn't even going to show the tiniest bit of respect to her team leader?

After far too long for Kareem's lungs, he made it back to the house of the venari and collapsed into the sand to wait for the rest of the pupils to arrive. Everyone looked like they had taken a dunk in the stream as they panted in the early morning heat. When the last pupil arrived, Hessa hopped down from her perch on a nearby railing.

Next time I expect all of you to complete that run in under thirty minutes. That was pathetic. Now get up so we can begin our daily exercises.

Everyone groaned, and Samira actually raised her hand. *Didn't we just complete our exercise for the day?*

Hessa looked at her like she had grown a second head before shouting, *Everyone, line up! Four rows of four and one row of three!*

She then proceeded to push them through several rounds of what she called "conditioning." It included press-ups, sit-ups, lunges, squats, running in place, dashing back and forth through the sand, and it finished with holding a straight form while resting forearms and toes on the ground for ten minutes. Most of them barely made it to three.

They collapsed again to the ground, panting as Hessa went and spoke with a venari that had come into the ring. Looking to the side, Kareem spotted Binita not far away, so he stood on shaking muscles and made his way over to her.

Hey, how's it going? he asked tentatively. She had an arm thrown over her eyes, and her dense curls were sticking out in a few places.

She grunted before saying, *Fantastic. Never better.*

Kareem didn't know what to follow that up with, but thankfully Hessa returned to the group with Amol this time. He was carrying what looked like a pile of wooden swords while Hessa dragged out a very large chest into the sand.

Everyone, come close and pay attention, she said, flipping the chest open. The wilted pupils became very interested in the contents of the chest. Kareem made his way closer and saw a multitude of obsidian weapons glinting in the light from above. All venari carried such weapons, as well as the warriors. The warriors preferred more battle-friendly weapons such as a spear or sword, while venari tended to stick with knives and daggers that could be hidden in human society.

I don't need any mind-reading abilities to know what many of you are thinking, Hessa said, looking around at a few confused faces that peered into the chest. Kareem only then realized he had no idea what Hessa's ability was.

Many of you know that venari don't use swords, spears, or bows like the warriors do. But you may not know that all venari train using all forms of weapons before going out on an assignment. While you may not carry a spear into human cities without drawing significant attention, you will be trained to defend yourself against various opponents. Venari must be prepared for any situation that may arise. We will demonstrate for you.

Hessa nodded to Amol, who grinned and plucked a sword that was as wide across as Kareem's palm. It was still light enough that it could be wielded with one hand, leaving the other free, and that's what Amol chose to do. Hessa chose two identical short swords and motioned for the group to back up. The pupils who just minutes ago claimed they were dying from exhaustion scrambled back to give them enough room. Kareem noticed the boy who had the electricity ability in his hands and looked at Hessa with a smug expression, only taking a single step back.

Hessa and Amol squared up, and Kareem realized how much smaller Hessa really was than Amol, yet her posture was that of someone ten feet tall. A slow smile slid over her own face.

Begin.

It happened quickly, Amol took one step, and Hessa took two. It looked like they were starting to dance when the grating sound of obsidian on obsidian echoed sharply. He didn't even see where their blades connected, but flashes of black stabbed and slashed in arcs around their bodies. Kareem was confused why Amol didn't grip the wide blade with two hands until he noticed Hessa doing everything to avoid his free hand.

It must be something to do with his ability, Kareem thought.

A girl in front of him was bobbing her head back and forth, and Kareem couldn't see, so he pushed past a few people to get a better view. Hessa and Amol were moving around each other in bursts of movement unmarked by hesitation. Amol had Hessa backing up, and he faked to the right before doubling back and bringing his blade down toward Hessa.

Kareem and the others gasped when she suddenly moved differently. Her body went hard to her left, and it looked like her image trailed behind her, as if her entire body were made of still-burning smoke. Amol's blade came right down on her shoulder, but the smoke-Hessa dissipated, and the real Hessa solidified faster than the eye could track to Amol's right. She kicked out toward his knees and had him stumbling in the sand. Amol only laughed and charged toward her while Hessa became twisting smoke again.

Amol and the smoke-Hessa swung and clashed, coming

together and breaking apart in a terrifying dance that could have ended tragically at any moment. Kareem didn't actually see when it happened, but one moment smoke-Hessa was swirling to Amol's left, and the next, she solidified so fast she stumbled and yelped as her ankle twisted. Kareem would've been on the ground in pain, but Hessa was already wrenching back, and he saw Amol's free hand had been clamped around her wrist.

Hessa shook her head as if trying to orient herself before smoking out again as Amol's blade came down. Again, somehow he managed to get a hand on her, and she solidified with a growl. Amol's teeth were clenched in an eager frenzy; his victory was in sight. He towered over Hessa and slammed his blade down fast. She had to throw up both of hers to catch his, forcing her down to one knee and leaving her vulnerable to his free hand. They both saw this, and Amol smiled as his hand shot out to grab her wrist. In the next breath, all Kareem saw was smoke and flashing obsidian. As Amol leaned his weight forward to reach for her, Hessa smoked out, dropping her weapons and putting Amol off balance. The smoke-Hessa lunged forward and solidified just in time to grab Amol's ankle, yanking up as he tilted forward. His whole body went crashing face-first into the sand as Hessa stood up amid her own smoke.

The pupils whooped and cheered at the display as Hessa offered a hand to Amol, who muttered something along the lines of "Show off." Hessa allowed a small, leonine smile as she turned to face the group.

Every fight will look different for each of you. You will learn your strengths and how to properly use your abilities to help you in that fight. But before we start incorporating your abilities into combat, you need a solid foundation for moving your body and wielding a weapon. I use Amol for this demonstration because it is a reminder that you may not always be able to rely solely on your abilities. Can anyone guess what Amol's ability was?

The man in question stood behind her with arms crossed and looked over the group.

A stunning ability? Ovi's voice questioned. Kareem spotted him on the other side of the group.

Amol nodded. *More than that,* he said. *I stun your ability itself with contact.*

A few pupils blanched at that, and Hessa nodded. *So today, we will start with the foundation. I will teach you the basic forms for a short sword. Everyone, please come and grab a wooden practice sword.*

As Kareem walked up to the front, he heard the boy with the electricity mutter something to his friend about being treated like babies. The other boy, who looked like he had never smiled a day in his life, flicked his eyebrows up in dull amusement.

Caden El Tain! Hessa called with a smile. *Thank you so much for volunteering to help with the demonstrations. Everyone else, please grab a sword and get into your lines.* The boy, Caden, looked like he wanted to hurtle his sword across the room, but stalked to the front where Hessa was.

Kareem wedged himself in with the others to grab a wooden sword from the pile up front. Just as he was about to grab one, a shoulder was pushing him out of the way, and long hair snapped in his eyes. He pulled back to see Zara had grabbed the sword he was reaching for. She gave him a look that said she thought higher of the bugs beneath her shoe and sauntered off toward Inaam and Faiza, hair swishing over her shoulders. In contrast to Zara, Inaam looked like she was always on the verge of a smile, like there was some secret joke she knew and you didn't. She looked at Kareem this way now as he grabbed a different sword and got back in line.

Kareem could have sworn the heat suddenly picked up in the room, but when he glanced up, the sun was just entering the space of open air above the training ring. Wiping the sweat from his brow and planting his feet in the sand, he listened to Hessa as she drove them through drill after drill as the sun swept over them.

I can't feel my legs.

At least you can feel your arms.

She's insane.

We'll definitely be dead by the end of the month.

Kareem listened to the mental chatter as he trudged mindlessly with the other pupils toward the dining hall. It wasn't until he got there that he realized he wasn't hungry yet despite the state of exhaustion his body was in. A tiny part of his mind contemplated skipping the afternoon classes to sleep. The logical and determined part of his mind quickly remedied the malfunction, and he was horrified he had even thought it was an option.

He spotted Zara in the dining room with a gaggle of other pupils, but there was no way she would converse with him unless she had to. Since he didn't see Ovi or Bonita either, he decided to head back to his room to get in some rest before the afternoon.

As he dragged himself through the halls, he reflected on how poorly the first two days were going. He had been given a team that wanted nothing to do with him and even less once they found out he was their leader. They had lost the initial skirmish, and none of them had seemed to amaze the older venari. Kareem had only seen Savar and Zaid briefly in passing, and neither had so much as glanced in his direction. The only bright spot had been meeting Aryan and Waqas.

There has to be some way to pull us together, he thought as he tried to block out the pain in his legs as he went up the stairs to the upper floor. At least two of the other teams already seemed to work together cohesively, even if they weren't seamless yet. Kareem was barely on speaking terms with his. The first place he ought to start with was his roommate. He could deal with Zara and Bonita later.

Pushing the door open to his room, he found Ovi sitting on his bed reading a book. Kareem instantly brightened. This was perfect.

Hi Ovi, Kareem said, coming into the room. *I'm glad you're here. Mind if we talk?* He was never one to avoid a conversation that needed to be had.

The other boy glanced up from his book, eyes barely over the edge. *Hm?* was all he said.

We just never got to talk as a team about the whole team leader thing and all that, Kareem said, sitting on his bed. Sleep called to him, but he forced himself to focus on Ovi instead.

Ovi shrugged a shoulder. *What is there to talk about? I saw you were selected. Congratulations.* He turned back to his book. He didn't sound ingenuine, but he wasn't enthusiastic either.

I think it would be best if we at least started acting like a team. Since, you know, we have to work together to win a skirmish. You do want to graduate, right? Kareem crossed his arms and leaned back against the wall.

Ovi exhaled through his nose and closed his book. Kareem got a glance at the title and saw it was a book on herbology. What could a venari use with an herbology text?

I can tell you're a nice guy, Ovi said, turning to him. *Yes, I do need to graduate, but I'm not getting my hopes up. None of us are alike at all, and we don't have any useful abilities. No offense.* He gave Kareem an awkward smile that looked more like a grimace. *And honestly, do you have any leadership experience? I know you were selected, but I don't see how you could be any better off than the rest of us.*

Kareem was at a loss for words, and Ovi took that as his agreement.

I'm not trying to be mean or anything, I just think attempting to be best friends is a waste of all of our time. I think we should just focus on our skills and learn as we go, and then just hope we are each better in our own right so we can come out on top with one of the skirmishes.

He said it so matter-of-factly that Kareem wondered if they

had talked about this behind his back. Kareem was too angry to speak now and just looked at his lap. It was true; he had never led anyone in his life. He was just about fourteen and didn't have much experience in anything, really. But he wouldn't use that as an excuse not to try. It was clear Ovi intended to be as resistant as possible to the idea of Kareem's leadership.

Good talk, Ovi said with a nod and pulled his book back into his lap as if they had been talking about the weather and not the future of their lives.

Kareem didn't bother saying another word. He was too frustrated. He spent the rest of his break facing the wall, pretending to sleep. He didn't want to admit, even to himself, that he was embarrassed he hadn't even considered that the others wouldn't *want* him to be their leader. Instead of mulling it over, he tried to at least be productive and get some sleep.

It didn't happen.

The afternoon consisted of three classes; human studies to teach them about human societies, how they operate, and how to blend in; abilities training to help them develop their own abilities and be effective with them; and mental conditioning to strengthen their minds. Kareem already knew much about human society. It was taught in primary school, and he studied up on it as much as possible. He didn't have too much difficulty with the abilities training either, as his ability was pretty straightforward. The instructor promised that he would be able to use his ability for longer and potentially at range, but Kareem felt comfortable with what he had. Zara was also in the same small group as him and had the opposite experience.

She spent the entire class in denial. Besides ignoring Kareem's very existence no matter how much he tried to speak with her, she also insisted to the instructor—a hardened older woman by the name of Tala—that her gift would only last a few seconds and that wouldn't ever change. Tala just shook her head and had the rest of the pupils demonstrate their gifts.

It was the last class that Kareem had the most trouble with. He had spent the last few years meditating for at least fifteen minutes each morning. He thought he did pretty well at it, but according to Laban, who was teaching the class, he had the mental control of a starving infant. They spent nearly two hours doing different mental exercises that consisted of balancing eggs on their heads while meditating, having projectiles thrown at them while meditating, and reciting the alphabet backward while having said projectiles thrown at them while meditating. Kareem wondered if there was a way to opt out of a class due to its ridiculousness. In what world would he need to recite the alphabet in reverse while an ubir was attacking him?

By the end of the day, he was frustrated and exhausted. His mind and body were fried, and the day had only gotten worse as it went on. Kareem had prepared for this for years, and within two days, he was already starting to doubt himself. It was a bitter thing when your dreams weren't as bright during the day as they were when you were asleep. When he got back to his room that evening, he didn't bother talking to Ovi and just fell into bed. Within minutes, he was sleeping.

CORONATION DAY

That was acceptable, Aryan. Veer, your turn, Tala said as she removed a board covered in mud from a table in the center of the room. She placed a single rock in the empty space while Veer got ready.

It had been two weeks since Kareem's venari training had begun, and he had fallen into a methodical, if not productive, routine. He spent his mornings beating his body into submission at Hessa's behest and the afternoons in windowless classrooms. All while being ignored by his teammates, no matter how hard he tried to get them to cooperate. This was one of many such afternoons with Tala and five other students working on enhancing their abilities. Throughout the last few weeks, Kareem had grown quite comfortable in this class while learning what he could about the others—whether Zara liked it or not. As usual, she knelt on the opposite side of the room and avoided eye contact with him.

Kareem watched as Veer, the boy who had sat with him, Aryan, and Samira on that first day with Hessa, stood and approached the table. Since they all had different abilities, each test had to be catered to them specifically. Today they were working on isolating their abilities. Kareem had already been tasked with sticking a large cloth to the wall but only allowed a small, one-inch circle to stick while the rest fell around it.

Veer's ability was something Kareem found quite deceptive, yet he could see its usefulness to a venari. The boy stepped up to the table, and his wide shoulders blocked Kareem's view. A moment later, he stepped to the side, and instead of a rock, a pile of Rhaptan shillings sat scattered in its place. He knew it would only last a few hours before reverting back to a rock.

Excellent, Tala said with an approving nod. She had shown to be stern on the outside but had glints of pride in her eyes when her pupils did well. Kareem wondered if she had children or even grandchildren in the city somewhere. *Zara, you're next,* she said as she removed the shillings from the table.

Zara stood, already with a frown on her face, as she walked toward the middle of the room. Tala had placed two small pots on either end, each with a small flower. They had already watched her attempt this once before with little success. She was supposed to lower the temperature just enough on half of the table to make the flower start to wilt. No more, no less.

Zara stood before the table, and only a breath went by, and Kareem could feel the cold air seeping toward this side of the room. At first, nothing happened to either flower, but the next moment they were both black and curled up. Kareem rubbed the skin on his arms.

Zara's eyes flicked up to Tala's. *As I said, that kind of control is not part of my ability. It doesn't get that specific.*

Tala lifted her chin. *Watch your tone, girl. I have been training abilities longer than your parents have been alive. Your ability is related not only to temperature, but to atmospheric control. If I tell you you can do something, then you can. You will try again next time.*

Zara shook her head but said nothing as she knelt back in her spot. Kareem swore she was fuming out of her nostrils and wasn't surprised when the heat in the room crept back up to its normal temperature quickly.

Mira, your turn, Tala said as she cleared away the flowers. She didn't replace them with anything this time as the small girl came to the middle of the room and faced the group. The first time he saw her, Kareem was sure she was little more than eleven years old, but she had stated she was nearing fifteen already.

The room watched raptly as they always did when Mira shifted. She held steady and looked like she was focusing on her breathing. Her only movement was the rise and fall of her gray uniform on her chest as she inhaled and exhaled.

Her eyes shifted first from dark brown to bright yellow-gold cat's eyes. They glowed brightly in the shadows of her face, sending shivers running up Kareem's spine.

One more step, Tala said quietly from where she stood by the door.

Mira gave a short nod and stretched her jaw as if to yawn. Her front teeth shifted slowly, growing to fill her mouth with two-inch-long canines. She held it for a second, and Kareem swore he saw a swath of dark fur ripple across her right hand before it disappeared.

Tala nodded. *Much better, Mira,* she said. Kareem had to agree, and the other pupils released a breath in unison. The first time Mira displayed her ability, a massive panther had suddenly taken the space of the small girl, its yowl sending Kareem's heart into a frenzy. Over the last two weeks, she had progressed rapidly to being able to isolate small changes instead. She reminded Kareem a little of Ovi, though. Quiet unless spoken to directly, and with a deadly ability underneath.

Kareem glanced to the side and saw another boy watching her with intense eyes. Idris, Kareem had gathered, was Caden's unsmiling friend. Something about him set Kareem on edge, and the few times he had tried to talk to him, Idris had merely looked at him with those intense eyes before moving on like no one had spoken.

Idris, you are the last to go, Tala said as Mira knelt in her spot next to Zara. Tala had placed two large beetles in the center of the table this time. Other than Mira's, Idris's ability was the only other one in the room that made him uncomfortable. He said his ability was influence, but how much influence was correlated to how big the thing he was trying to influence was. The smaller the thing, the easier it was to control. So far, Tala had only been having him test this on beetles or other small insects. Kareem wasn't too inclined to see what it would do to a person.

Idris stood and walked to the table. He just looked at the two beetles that were walking aimlessly in the center. One of the beetles started to move in a zig-zag motion, its movements too perfect to be of its own volition.

Tala was nodding slowly in the corner, watching the beetles with the rest of the room. The one stayed on its aimless path while the other made its movements back and forth in Idris's direction.

Suddenly the beetle made a small noise, and it was dashing across the table toward the other. Kareem watched in horror as one beetle attacked another with a vicious, high-pitched shriek. Their exoskeletons made it hard to see what was happening, but one was flipped over and started shrieking even louder, the sound piercing in the small room.

Idris's face didn't change from its normal stony expression, but Kareem thought he saw something like delight in those intense eyes of his.

That's enough! Tala snapped.

Idris's focus broke, and the shrieking beetles stopped. One lay unmoving as the other meandered as if dazed. Across the room, Zara and Veer were wincing, and Mira had her hands over her ears.

That was unnecessary, Tala said as she stalked across the room. She swept the beetles into a small bag. *Idris, if you are unable to keep the thing you influence from attacking another, then you have no control at all. I expect better results next time.* She looked around the room with a huff. *That's enough for the day, you are free to leave a few minutes early.*

Zara was the first one up and hurrying out the door. Kareem had decided in a split second that now would be the best time to try to talk to her. There would be almost no one in the halls for a few more minutes. Without saying goodbye to Aryan, Kareem hurried and followed Zara out the door.

Zara! he said as he got out in the hall. Her longer legs gave her a bit of an advantage as she stalked down the hallway, headed to the south wing. *Zara, hold on a moment,* he repeated.

She wasn't turning around, and Kareem had to speed up to get to her. When he got close, he reached out and snagged her wrist.

That was a mistake.

Zara immediately spun around and shoved him in the chest. Hard. Her long hair whipped around her as well, and Kareem thought for the hundredth time how impractical it was for a venari to have hair like that.

Who exactly do you think you are? she seethed, her eyes as cold as ice, daring him to respond.

Kareem was momently enraged and seemed to have lost his words, just as he had with Ovi. Zara, however, didn't give him enough time to respond and spun away, continuing down the hall. Kareem glared after her but didn't follow. She was really starting to get on his nerves.

Barely muffled laughter came from behind him, and Kareem turned to find Caden and Idris coming his way down the hall. The former was looking between Kareem and Zara's retreating back with thinly veiled mirth, a few sparks of electricity jumping around his fingers. The latter just looked Kareem from head to toe as they brushed past him. Caden's shoulder took Kareem in the arm, making him spin partway around. Kareem sucked in through his teeth, and it took everything in him not to stick Caden to the wall.

Thankfully Aryan called his name, coming the same way Caden and Idris had with Veer. *What was all that about?* he asked, looking at the two boys. Veer had stopped with him, and they looked a mixture of concern and annoyance.

Kareem took a breath. *Nothing, just a bunch of big-headed people.*

Veer pursed his lips. *My dad says people with big abilities tend to have large egos.*

It certainly applies to them, Kareem said, nodding down the hall.

Are you headed to the festival later? Aryan asked, changing the subject. Kareem had honestly forgotten about the holiday. It was Coronation Day, the day every year Rhaptans celebrated the coronation of their queen. There would be food, dancing, and drinking for those of age throughout the city from midday until tomorrow morning. Kareem was never one for such silly things and usually only went to watch Akilah and her friends. Venari didn't get the day off like most of the city, but they were free to do what they chose outside of training.

I doubt it, Kareem said, still agitated by his run-in with Zara. *Hey, I'm going to be late for my next class. I'll see you guys later.* He headed back to the north wing. Truthfully, he wouldn't have been late, but he couldn't concentrate on the holiday right now. He felt lost every time he saw the other teams spending time together and training together when his was such a frazzled mess. Why did his team need to make things so difficult?

He unclenched his jaw and made his way to his least favorite class of the day. As usual, Laban reminded him he had the mental control of something humiliating like a chimpanzee with a sugar high or a rabid dog in a hurricane. Binita happened to be in the same class and was defter at avoiding him than her other team-mates. Also, unlike Kareem, Laban praised her like she was the heir to the throne. Kareem didn't bother trying to talk to her. He felt fed up with his team and, by the end of class, decided he needed help.

They hadn't seen much of Neelan since the first day. He stopped by their rooms every now and again and told Kareem his guidance would come later during their assignments, but he was always open to talk if they needed. It took a bit of wandering around, but Kareem finally found the venari's room somewhat closer to the training ring.

Thankfully, the door was propped open, and Neelan was digging around in a bag on his bed. Most of the older venari had single rooms, and Kareem felt a little jealous as he knocked on the frame.

Neelan looked up and smiled, his green eyes bright in the dimness. *Kareem! It's good to see you. Come in.* Despite the single bed, the room was still small like most venari rooms, and Kareem only took two steps before he was firmly inside. *What can I help you with?* Neelan asked, still digging in the bag.

I wanted your advice on something, Kareem said, thinking about how to formulate his question.

Team troubles? Neelan asked. He made a noise of surprise and smiled as he pulled something out of his bag. It was a mbira, a small wooden board with metal tines set in rows to be plucked to make music. It looked haphazardly built at best. Neelan glanced over at him. *You play?*

Kareem shook his head. *And yeah, it was about my team. How did you know?*

Neelan sat on his bed and plucked one of the tines with his thumb. It made a flat, ugly sound that had Neelan frowning. *It's quite common, especially for new pupils,* he said, digging around in his bag again. He produced a small metal bar that he started prying up the offending tune with.

Kareem sighed and leaned against the wall. *We are doing horri-*

ble. They've hardly talked to me since the first day, and some of them think I'm not fit to be the leader. Do you know why I was selected?

Neelan shook his head as he continued to adjust the mbira. *Savar decides those things, but trust me, if he chose you, then there is a good reason for it. Savar doesn't make mistakes like that. Your Tejas's brother, right?*

Kareem nodded. *You know him?*

Neelan gave a wry smile. *Yeah, he's a couple of years younger than me, but we used to spar during his training days. I always lost,* he added with a breathy laugh. *You must then know it was much different for us when we went through training before all the changes were made.*

Yes, Kareem said, thinking back to when Tejas first told him he wouldn't be working solo assignments anymore. Tejas had been bewildered and excited, and Kareem realized his older brother must have been lonely all those years working alone. *I was pretty young when the changes started, but yes, you never had teams, right?*

Right, Neelan said. He seemed happy with one of the tines and worked on adjusting another. *I can't tell you the number of times I wished I didn't have to do the things I did alone. Even if it was with someone I hated, at least there would be another person, another Anunnaki out there with me. When I was really young, before I ever started training, we heard about a venari that never made it home. It was a former neighbor of my cousin's. He went out on assignment like he always did but never returned home in time. It took months to figure out what happened to him, but they finally did. He got into a scuffle with an ubir with a pretty nasty poison ability. The ubir got away, and the venari was too weak to make it back to a portal. He died alone in the woods somewhere in Northern Canada.*

Kareem didn't know what to say, and he realized he was having that problem a lot lately. In all his years of wishing that he were the greatest venari, he never really thought too much about what would happen if he got hurt, really hurt. Would Tejas come looking for him if he never returned home?

Neelan glanced up at him, noting the forlorn expression on his face. *The bright side,* he said, *is that you don't have to worry about that. You have people who will be with you at all times. Your team is meant to be your family, not just a bunch of people to take charge of. Try treating them like you would your siblings. As their leader, it's your duty to care for them just as much, if not more than they are to care for you.*

But how do I do that if they won't even talk to me? Kareem asked, feeling frustrated again. He crossed his arms over his chest.

Neelan shrugged enigmatically. *That's for you to figure out. For now, I would relax and enjoy the evening. Go out and enjoy the festival while you can. The future will only get harder. There!* Neelan tossed the metal bar onto the bed and held up the mbira. It looked the same, but he gave Kareem a curious smile before plucking a few of the tines. A simple tune echoed out from the bits of metal, and Kareem could only wonder how Neelan made music from a lump of what looked like junk. He didn't say it, but it was actually quite peaceful, and he felt himself relax at the simple string of notes.

Kareem's brows suddenly furrowed. *Neelan,* he said, *if you don't mind my asking, what is your ability?*

Neelan stopped playing and looked up with a glint in his green eyes. *Can't you tell? It's music. I can play anything and have perfect pitch.* He looked down lovingly at the mbira in his hands.

Kareem's brows rose this time. *That's an... odd ability for a venari. I assume you weren't tapped and joined on your own?*

Neelan laughed out loud at that. *Yes, I almost had to beg Savar to join, but that's a story for another day.* He nodded toward the door. *Go enjoy yourself for the evening.*

As Kareem bid his goodbyes and headed down the hall, he could hear the sound of the mbira and its little tune coming from Neelan's room.

THE SUN WAS ALREADY SETTING by the time Kareem got to the central plaza. It wasn't far from the house of the venari, and that was his only reason for going. He heard the noise the moment he stepped outside and was accosted on all sides by it once he got to the plaza. Aurastone lamps were on every corner, ready to combat the dark at a moment's notice, and the massive Aurastone in the center was already glowing softly. The Grand Hall to his right was lit with braziers and sconces as well to add to the festivity. The perimeter of the plaza was filled with row after row of vendors selling specialty foods and goods for the holiday. The center of the plaza and around the large Aurastone were already filled with people dancing, each wearing more colorful clothing than the next person. He could hear thousands of beads rattling on the necks of the dancers from clear across the crowd.

Kareem had no interest in dancing and turned toward the rows of vendors. When they were as tightly packed as they were tonight, it almost felt like entering the halls of a building, the crowds squeezing in the narrow lanes. Spiced vegetables and fruits covered in delicate sugars were displayed at every booth. Several sellers were out parading their wares of fine jewelry and rare human clothes to every person that walked by. Most looked over Kareem and assumed he was too young to have any money, though, which was fine with him. He wondered if he would see his family here. He knew Tejas had already returned and left again on another assignment, but his parents and sister could be here somewhere.

Kareem spent nearly two hours wandering around the booths, looking at items but never buying anything other than a few small things to eat. It would be enough to satisfy him for several days, but there was one booth in particular he was looking for. At one point, he passed closer to the center of the plaza and saw a crowd had grown near the steps of the Grand Hall. The Aurastones in the area flashed brighter for a moment, and Kareem knew there was only one person who could do that. His guess was confirmed when hundreds of people started cheering as a figure in red robes and turquoise and gold beads in her hair descended from the Hall.

Kareem had seen the queen on various occasions, as all Rhaptans had. To the people, she always appeared radiant and loving, eager to see her Anunnaki as much as they were to see her. But to him, she was a figure he only ever saw at a distance, a lofty figure with which he doubted he would ever interact with. Kareem knew if he looked hard enough, he could find... there. Off to the right, but not too far from her side, was Zaid. In contrast to the queen, he always looked like he was at a crossroads of boredom and annoyance during events like these. But as the queen's consort, he was expected to be with her during these events. There would surely be a speech soon, but Kareem didn't bother getting closer to listen.

Turning back into the rows of vendors, Kareem finally found the one he was looking for. In a corner stall, a small booth sat with blue leaves hanging from the side and a gaggle of people waiting around it eagerly. Inside, a small man was shaking something in a bowl, and Kareem's mouth started to water. He got in line with the others. Before long, he had slices of melon on a stick covered in sweet cream and rolled in some of the hottest spices he had ever tasted.

Just as he was about to take a bite, he saw the top of a familiar head.

Kareem! Akilah shouted, her high-pitched voice making his brain wince. Her beaded braids clacked around her chin as she came running over to him with a group of her friends.

Where are Mama and Father? Kareem asked, looking around. *You're not alone, are you?*

Her friends giggled. *I'm almost ten, Kareem. And I have my friends, so I'm not technically alone.* They all giggled again as if it was the funniest thing in the world. *Aren't you supposed to be training or something?*

It would be just like her to not even miss her brother after not having seen him for two weeks. To be fair, she was used to only seeing Tejas once in a long while, so two weeks was nothing for her.

I am free to do as I please in the evenings, he said, tilting his stick of melon so the sweet cream wouldn't run over his fingers. *Also, it's late. Shouldn't you be in bed? Do you even have any money?*

Akilah rolled her eyes and groaned, her friends looking at her knowingly. *It's a holiday,* she said, as if that was an excuse. *And I was actually going to see if you had any—*

Hold on, Kareem said, shushing her. He had just been about to take a bite of his melon when he spotted *another* familiar head. In contrast, this one sent his blood boiling immediately. He made a decision at that moment and dug out a few shillings and deposited them in Akilah's hand. *Don't tell Mama I gave you that. Now leave me alone,* he said, pushing past the kids. He vaguely heard Akilah's shrieks of laughter with her friends as they ran off. Kareem had already forgotten.

Kareem was shouldering past a few other people waiting outside the blue leaf stall to a small sitting area to the left. Before he got there, Zara spotted him, and her face quickly went from smiling at Inaam and Faiza to blistering annoyance. She stood up, about ready to hurry away, but Kareem got there first.

Can you just—

No, Kareem, she said loudly. *Stop trying to talk to me.* She moved to step around him, but he blocked her path. Faiza and Inaam were instantly up, their food forgotten on the ground.

Just give me two minutes, Kareem said hotly. *I only want to talk. You owe me that.*

Zara's mouth popped open. *Owe you?* she asked in disbelief.

Faiza watched Kareem but spoke to Zara. *Do you want me to remove him?* Kareem knew she could and remembered how she had rammed into him during the first skirmish. He was sure her ability had something to do with weighing as much as an elephant despite her toned form.

Zara crossed her arms and shook her head. *No, just give us two minutes,* she said, voice dripping in disdain. Inaam and Faiza walked a little ways away, the latter glaring daggers at Kareem. *Well?* she said, lifting her eyebrows expectantly.

Kareem pushed back his shoulders. He wouldn't be cowed by her. *I've let you and the others sulk for two weeks now*—Zara's eyes widened in outrage—*but you have to agree that this is not the way for us to succeed.*

Zara actually barked out a laugh. *The absolute audacity...* She seemed at a loss for words as she stared at him. *Do you actually think we are sulking, Kareem? Tell me seriously, how spoiled were you as a child? Because the complete blindness to your own faults is... is crazy!* She threw up her hands right as a cheer came from the crowd in the plaza, drowning out her exclamation.

What are you talking about? Kareem shouted back at her. He flung an arm out—the one not holding the stick of melon. *I have been trying to get our team together since the first day, and you all run away the first chance you can get. Are you so against graduating? Because working together is the only way we can do that.* Kareem was seething.

Why, for the love of Rhapta, would we want to work with you?! Zara shouted, stepping closer. People around them ignored them and just pushed past.

Kareem inhaled, but Zara cut him off.

No! Zara said, holding her palms up to stop him. *You don't get to tell us what to do. From the first day,* she said, mocking him, *you have been rude, bossy, and self-centered. You treat us like you're an old military commander, and we are your groveling little warriors eager to do your bidding.*

I'm rude?! Kareem stared openmouthed at her, but she kept going and stepped closer, those icy eyes narrowed at him.

You act like your better than everyone, she said, *and as if we couldn't possibly be as good of a venari as you and your macho self-discipline. Just because we don't do as you say doesn't mean we aren't trying.*

She was now standing close enough that he could smell something sweet, an almond-vanilla scent coming off her. Was she wearing perfume?! It was another ridiculously impractical thing for a venari, but it was probably not the best time to bring it up.

I don't think I'm better than everyone, Kareem said quietly, still scowling. *I just think that—*

See?! Zara exclaimed. *Everything is about you! What you want us to do, what you think, what you need. You, you, you! You were clearly disappointed in who you got for your team, so you might as well go be a team by yourself!*

Kareem was angry, angrier than he had been in a long time, and if he could just stomp down the emotions in his head, everything would work out fine. He just needed to find a way to get Zara to understand. She was wrong about him. She had to be...

He wasn't like that, was he?

He opened his mouth, but no words came out. He didn't know the right thing to say. Zara, on the other hand, had said everything apparently, because she shook her head and pushed past him and into the crowd.

Even once she was gone, Kareem found he still didn't know what he could have said to convince her. A sick, bitter feeling wormed under his skin, and he didn't know what it meant.

Looking down, he saw the sweet cream from the melon had dribbled down all over his hand, the spicy flakes having long fallen off. He threw the ruined thing on the ground and left the plaza.

DEEP WATER

All Kareem knew when he woke up was that it was going to be a bad day. Before the blurriness had gone from his eyes, he was already thinking of when he could go back to sleep. It was unlike him to sleep later than Ovi, but the other boy was almost totally dressed by the time Kareem got out of bed.

After his fight with Zara, he had come back to the house, ignoring the rest of the Coronation Day celebrations that raged all night. He couldn't stop thinking about what she had said. She made it sound like he was a brutish bully who only cared about winning. It wasn't true. He had never been like that. Self-discipline was something that he cultivated throughout his childhood. How else was he supposed to achieve anything?

He and Ovi didn't speak as they made their way down to the training ring. The first rays of light were peeking through the empty space above the ring as this year's pupils gathered there. Kareem absently wondered where the older pupils trained. There was usually a few additional years' worth of pupils, but the youngest were in the ring alone every morning.

Kareem trudged through the sand, an ache already building in his shoulders. The weapon's training from the day before had left him sore all over, in addition to the usual exhaustion he was beginning to become familiar with after mornings with Hessa. The venari woman had her hood up this morning, but her steps were quick and light like a cheetah as she stalked into the ring.

They went through their usual torture. A run around the entire city to warm up usually had one or two students vomiting in the sand when they returned. This was followed by a myriad of exercises meant to obliterate individual muscles. Kareem took his anger out on his own body, pushing himself harder and harder until he was sure he would pass out. He didn't.

When they were finished with those, most crumpled into the sand, but Kareem paced, hands on hips, while trying to get air back into his lungs. He couldn't help but glare in Zara's direction, but she was whispering to Inaam and Faiza in a circle. Ovi and Aryan were nodding to each other; words exchanged over shared physical misery. Kareem didn't realize they were friends and wondered if Ovi was complaining to Aryan about him.

Before he got a chance to stomp over there and ask, Hessa addressed the group. Since the demonstration a few weeks before, Hessa hadn't shown her ability again. Kareem still couldn't help but watch for smoke every time she moved.

Pupils! she said, coming closer. *Follow me. We will be doing something a little different today.* She turned on her heel, and the group scrambled to keep up with her. Amol and Laban were both with them today and followed behind to watch for any stragglers. Hessa walked to the back of the ring and ducked under one of the rails to the hallway on the other side. Heading down, Kareem thought they were headed out the rear entrance, but she turned and unlocked a door on the right side of the hall before heading inside.

Kareem was in the middle of the group between Mira and Tarun, and they stepped inside and found a staircase headed down in the dimness. There were small Aurastones affixed to the walls that gave off little light as they descended. Kareem was confused when they kept going down and down, much further than he thought the building sat in the ground. In fact, the air started to get cooler, and Kareem realized they were going underground.

His suspicions were confirmed when they finally got to the bottom and stepped into a vast chamber held up by massive limestone pillars set at intervals throughout the room as if on a grid. The entire city had a series of cisterns that collected rainwater and funneled it wherever it was needed before being sanitized. This looked to be one of such chambers, but Kareem hadn't realized the venari had been using it as a training room.

More Aurastones were affixed to the walls along the length of the huge room. Toward the far end, Kareem could see a twenty-five-foot gap in the floor spanning horizontally across the room. If he remembered correctly, there would be water down there that was collected through tiny aqueducts that drained into this room. On the far wall was another door similar to the one they came out of.

Once everyone was inside, Hessa turned to face the group. *Today, we are going to see how well your teams are doing supporting one another.*

Kareem internally groaned, clenching his teeth hard enough to cause a twinge of pain in his jaw.

Your teams will complete three separate tasks today. Each member will need to complete the task. You will also not be allowed to use your abilities. The room audibly gasped, and Hessa looked each of them sternly in the eye from within the shadows of her hood.

Samira raised her hand. *Is this going to count toward the skirmishes we need to complete?*

Hessa shook her head. *This is just part of your training. As a team, you should be leaning on each other for support.*

Kareem wanted to scream. Irritation started ticking inside his head like a bomb counting down. He wanted the class to be over—

and the rest of the day—so he could go back to his room. The room agitated him, the pupils agitated him, and even Hessa was getting on his nerves. Why did she have to pick today to do this? He wanted to be as far from Zara and his other teammates as possible since they wanted to be just as far from him, clearly.

Your three tasks will start with a simple rope climb, followed by carrying a pillar across the room, and will end with walking across a bridge blindfolded. Kareem swore he heard the mental groaning of the other students. Only Hessa would call those things simple. He just needed to get through the next hour and could skip the rest of the afternoon.

They were taken off to the left, where someone had affixed five ropes to the ceiling. On closer inspection, the room wasn't as tall as he had originally thought. The shadows made it look bigger. At the top of the ropes, five small bells were attached. Each of the teams congregated together and stood in a line before the ropes.

Kareem had decided he wouldn't help his teammates today. If they were so against his leadership, then so be it. He would give them what they asked for and leave them alone. He stood with crossed arms while waiting for Hessa to tell them to begin. When Kareem didn't immediately say anything, the others looked around, wondering who would go first.

Binita finally spoke. *Are we supposed to be in order or something?*

Zara just shrugged, her mood only marginally better than Kareem's. Binita looked around, unsure, but stood at the beginning of the line. Kareem, Ovi, and Zara filed in behind her. Kareem just kept his head down and waited silently with the others. When Hessa shouted for the teams to begin, Binita dashed over to the rope before her, jumped, and grabbed hold of it.

She didn't move from there.

The other teams started shouting at their climbing teammates, some encouraging and others in some frenzied panic as if speed were of the utmost importance. Hessa never mentioned a winner or loser as an option, but many students saw otherwise.

Kareem and his team just watched Binita awkwardly hold the rope. She moved her limbs oddly, trying to find a way to keep the rope still while climbing up. Out of their group, she was the skinniest, and her thin arms seemed counterproductive to any attempt at strength. Binita herself seemed to disagree as she finally released one arm to grip higher on the rope. She made a shimmying motion with her feet up as well and managed to get up a little higher. She continued to do this until her grip slipped when she was almost to the top. She landed with a painful thud on the ground below.

The other teams were shouting, and Kareem noticed one of them was almost as quiet as theirs, but their members were doing much better on their task, with their second member almost done. As soon as Binita got out of the way, Kareem marched forward and gripped the rope, pulling himself up. It was difficult, but the anger boiling under his skin gave him a burst of energy that had him pulling himself higher. It took less time than he expected before he rang the bell and dropped to the ground, feet stinging as he landed.

Ovi went next and hardly made halfway before letting go and tumbling to the ground. Zara didn't even look like she tried before she grabbed on, shook her head, and let go. Hessa watched over the teams like a hawk, missing nothing as each bell was rung and each pupil dropped to the ground. Kareem didn't need any confirmation to know that if it had been a competition, they would have lost.

The next task was even worse. On the other side of the room, giant pieces of limestone nearly half the size of a cart were gathered in a pile, a graveyard for broken pillars. Each team was to carry one of the boulders from one side of the room and back. It seemed simple, but the boulders were beyond heavy and awkward to hold. Kareem's team didn't speak to each other than to say *I'm slipping!* They managed to drop the boulder no less than four times before they finished, well after the other teams.

By this time, Kareem's agitation was coming to a peak. There wasn't much more that he could handle. His team was *failing* at the first moment he refused to help, and they still didn't want him to be their leader. He could see them watching the other teams, all of which were doing better than them. At this rate, their whole team would be kicked out and banned from becoming venari. He wondered if that was what they were aiming for.

They all walked to the back of the room, where the gap in the floor started to seem much wider. Kareem saw he was correct and found the space was filled with still water below. Small pipes must have been at either end toward the bottom to funnel water in. Along the gap were five very narrow boards to get to the other side and the opposite door.

Kareem and his team stepped forward, and he caught Ovi stepping back with a shudder when he saw the water. Kareem gave him a look, and Ovi turned him wide eyes. *I can't swim!* he whispered intently. Zara and Binita spun around.

Seriously? Zara said. *This is a bad time to say that. On second thought, we're going to lose anyway, so you might as well just jump in.*

Binita turned her a scathing look. *You're not going to fall in,* she said to Ovi. *Either way, you'll float if you do. I'm a really good swimmer, so I would know.*

Kareem could only sigh. If he tried to speak, he'd say something he'd regret later.

All right, teams! Hessa yelled once they all got close. *Line up before one of the boards. I will be passing around blindfolds and checking to make sure you have tied them securely. Each member must cross the board to the other side. As a reminder, you cannot use your abilities at any time.*

Just as before, Binita went first, tying a black cloth handed to her by Hessa around her eyes. Ovi stood behind her, shaking imperceptibly in line. Amol and Laban crossed one of the boards to wait on the other side while Hessa stayed with a pile of black cloths for each pupil. When Hessa shouted for them to begin, five pupils stepped forward unsteadily onto the boards, each with arms out for balance.

A few of the other teams started yelling directions to their wobbly teammates, coaching them to stay on the board by inching to the left or right. Binita was tentative, moving slowly across the board. A few times, it looked like she would topple into the water, but she made it to the other side relatively easily. On both sides of her, Aryan and Faiza got to the other side safely as well. Two more pupils made it across without falling into the water.

Ovi was up. By the looks of him, he was headed straight to his grave, his shoulders hunching in more than usual. Hessa handed him a black cloth, and his shaking fingers could barely tie the knot. When Hessa shouted to begin, Ovi froze. To his left and right, Samira and Inaam had stepped onto their boards, if slowly. Their teams were coaching them across, but Ovi stayed frozen.

You must complete the task, Ovi, Hessa called. Some of the other pupils muffled their laughter at seeing Ovi too scared to cross.

Just go! Zara whispered to him, glancing at the other pupils.

Ovi stepped forward onto the board. His whole body started shaking then, making the board rattle in place.

This was going to end badly.

Samira was almost across, and Inaam was about halfway. Still, no other pupils had fallen in by the time Ovi took his next few steps. He basically shuffled his feet forward, half crouched, and never really removed his feet from the boards. He was about halfway when he wobbled and caught himself, freezing in place.

This is hard to watch, Zara said, more to herself than anyone.

To the side, Caden was waiting in line for Inaam to finish. He saw Ovi frozen on the board again and nudged Idris behind him, grinning.

Hey Ovi! he shouted. *Your board is breaking. You might want to hurry up!*

Ovi whipped his head to the side at the sound of his name, causing him to wobble again.

That's not true, Ovi! Binita shouted. *Come toward me!*

Ovi's head swiveled in her direction, and he took a tentative step, nearly missing the board when he put his foot down.

Ovi, hurry! To your left more! Caden shouted, laughing with the other pupils.

Kareem's irritation was beginning to look a lot like someone in particular. *He's messing with you, Ovi!* Kareem shouted finally, glaring at Caden.

No, no! Ovi, you're going to fall! Caden added.

Stop! both Kareem and Zara shouted at Caden, but it was too late. Ovi was teetering wildly on the board, having swung his head back and forth, unsure of which way was forward. The whole room held its breath, waiting to see if he righted himself, but Kareem's stomach condensed into a hard knot as Ovi spun too far, throwing his arms out, and then he was midair. It was silent for a single moment before he plunged into the dark water below.

One of the pupils screamed, and someone else started shouting, but Kareem's vision had gone red as Caden laughed hysterically. Kareem reacted as if on instinct. All of his agitation and anger from the last few weeks spiraled down to a single point where Caden's face was. Kareem's feet were moving as he thundered toward Caden and didn't stop until he slammed his arms around Caden's middle. He felt the woosh of air leave Caden's lungs, cutting his laugh short. A moment later, icy water surrounded them in a roar.

Kareem hardly knew what he was doing, other than tackling Caden seemed the best way to deal with the boiling anger under his skin. Caden immediately shoved away from him, frantically kicking and punching his limbs. Kareem faintly remembered that if

Caden decided to use his ability, they would both be dead in an instant. Water and electricity were a lethal combination. The thought that Caden would only hurt himself if he used his ability had Kareem slamming a fist as hard as he could into what he assumed was Caden's face. It was too dark to see, and bubbles erupted around them at their splash, but Kareem's fist connected with something, and fingers lashed out in his direction.

He kicked up toward the surface. His own lungs were starting to burn, and he imagined Caden's were much worse. It was difficult to find *up* other than to let himself rise in what he thought was the right direction. His head burst through the surface, and he gulped down air, soothing his lungs.

There was a cacophony of mental chatter, but he didn't pay attention to what they were saying. A hand with the strength of a god suddenly plunged down, grabbing the collar of his shirt, and hauled him out of the water like he was nothing more than a rag doll. Kareem sputtered and tried to wipe the water from his eyes. When he did, he found Laban looming over him, his face enraged. Kareem heard a yelp and saw Amol was doing the same to Caden.

Kareem didn't have time to speak before Laban shoved him across the remaining stretch of the room toward the rear door. He coughed and sputtered, dripping water everywhere as Laban pushed him through the door and barked at him to climb the steps. It was an identical stairwell to the one they had come in through, and Kareem entered the first floor of the house. Laban grabbed him by the collar and dragged him the rest of the way up the stairs, down the labyrinthine halls to his room.

When they got to his door, Kareem turned a hot glare to the venari, but Laban only looked back at him with a steely gaze as he let go of his collar.

Don't look at me, Laban said. *You're the one with the self-control of a cat about to be bathed.*

A bitter feeling twisted inside Kareem, and he shot back, *I have better self-control than any of them!* He flung a hand down the hall, indicating the other pupils. His breath was coming fast and deep. *I have been preparing myself for years. They're the ones who—*

No, Laban said loudly, his frown filling up his long face. *You try to beat yourself and others into submission. That's pain, Kareem, not discipline. If you knew anything about self-control, you would know that pain, anger, and force are balanced with compassion, love, and gentleness. You need to have both to gain any level of self-mastery.*

Kareem only glared down at his feet, his heart thrumming in his chest as he continued to drip water onto the floor.

You are confined to your room until told otherwise.

Thirty minutes later, Kareem was lying in dry clothes on his bed; an arm flung over his eyes. His heart was still too active in his chest to fall asleep, so he lay there fuming.

He hated Caden. He hated his team. He hated Laban more than the rest, though. The thought that he could be right made the fire in his chest burn hotter. He had spent as long as he could remember wanting to become venari. He had done everything he thought he needed to, and he was failing worse than all of them. He refused to allow tears to prick the back of his eyes, but he failed at that too.

The door opened, and Kareem heard feet shuffle inside, accompanied by wet squelching.

Hi.

Kareem grunted in response. He didn't want to remove his arm yet. He listened while Ovi got changed and sat on his own bed. He thought the other boy had fallen asleep, but he spoke suddenly, if quietly.

Thanks, by the way.
For what?
Drowning Caden.

Kareem sat up in alarm. Caden hadn't—Ovi was giving him a sly grin.

Kareem gave him a wry smile back. *He had it coming.* Ovi nodded, and they just sat there a moment. Kareem was back to not knowing what to say, so he just went with, *You okay?*

Ovi nodded. *Yeah, Binita jumped in and pulled me out.* His eyes were wide in amazement as he stared down at his bed. *She wasn't kidding; she's like a fish.*

Kareem couldn't help but laugh a little, wondering if Binita could give herself gills. *You really never learned how to swim?*

Ovi shook his head this time. His short hair was still damp and glinted in the Auralight. *My aunt and uncle are pretty protective.* When Kareem didn't say anything, he continued. *My parents died in the Battle of Rhapta five years ago, so my aunt and uncle took me in. They've always been very against violence and fighting, but even more so after the battle. So they never let me do anything dangerous, either. I think they were afraid I'd get hurt.*

Kareem sat quietly for a moment. No wonder Ovi was always skittish; he was never allowed to experience things and was probably told the world was a dangerous place. Kareem cocked his head. *What do they think about your ability, then?*

Never told them, Ovi said, leaning back. *Well, until I was tapped to be venari—it never even happens anymore, but of course it had to be me. I had just told them I was a dud for a few years. They loved me all the same, but when I got tapped, I had to tell them why. They were angry at first, but then they stopped speaking to me altogether.*

Kareem was dumbstruck. He really didn't know what to say now. How could a parent—even a guardian—be angry at their child for things they have no control over? His own parents would have loved him no matter his ability or profession.

Ovi caught his expression and shrugged. *I don't have a choice now. Besides, venari training is the best way for me to figure out how not to hurt someone. Even if I tried to fail and chose some other career, nothing would help me control my ability. Also,* he added, *I don't think I could face them if I saw them here in the city. If I'm venari, I'll be gone all the time.* He looked down at his lap, but he didn't cry. It was like this was an old sadness, something he'd already accepted.

What, Kareem started, still at a loss, *would you want to do instead? If you could?*

Ovi brightened a little. *I like botany. Nature, plants, like old human healers before their societies started advancing. It's kind of like a magic in itself.*

Kareem was saved from answering by a knock at the door. He got up to answer it, and Binita stood there in the doorway in dry clothes. She tilted to the side, looking in. *I came to check on Ovi.* Kareem moved to the side to let her in.

You look alive. That's good, she said when she saw Ovi on his bed. Kareem immediately noticed how Ovi's eyes were glued to her as she poked around the room.

Yeah, thanks for that, Ovi said.

You should really learn how to swim, she replied, frowning as she peered at the books piled on his shelf and then at Kareem's side of the room in pristine condition.

He nodded. *I'll work on that. What happened after I left?*

Binita shrugged. *Not much. Tarun fell in as well, but everyone else made it across. There were no winners, so...*

All three of them nodded, none of them wanting to say how poorly they were doing.

Well, I'll get going. Glad to see you're not dead. She turned and headed toward the door, where Kareem was still standing. Just before she left, she punched him lightly on the shoulder. *That was good, boss, even if you're in a load of trouble.*

Kareem nodded, words having failed him for the thousandth time. She was down the hall before he remembered to shut the door. As he got back into bed, Kareem realized the welling agitation he had been feeling had eased, if just a little.

CHAPTER 8

A HELPING HAND

Kareem walked through the northeastern streets of Rhapta, taking his time as he wound through the plazas with their fountains and statues in the center, many of them still latent by decorations from the Coronation Day celebration two weeks ago. Children were out playing in the streets this evening, parents lounging nearby.

He turned right into one of the larger plazas. If he had gone a little further, the route would have taken him to his parents' house. He had seen them only a week before for an evening meal, but he had kept the conversation light, telling them only the barest details of his training.

He certainly didn't mention the fight with Caden.

Tejas had assuredly heard about what happened but hadn't brought it up, at least yet. Kareem had been brought to Savar's office the following morning and had stood before the old venari's desk in a distressing silence while he finished writing in his ledger. The conversation included Kareem wanting to melt into the floor at the frowning disappointment of Savar as he recited all of the things that he had done wrong and why he would not be doing them in the future. Waqas, Aryan's brother, had said he got off easy when he saw him in the dining hall later that day. Kareem had to agree because he was half expecting to be expelled from venari training altogether.

He had also received a week's worth of punishment, having to get up early to clean latrines and sweep leaves from the roof. In the afternoons, after his classes, he was required to rake the sand in the training ring and was then confined to his room for the evening. He assumed Caden had the same punishment, but he had been trying to avoid the larger boy as much as his classes would allow. But based on the hostile looks from Caden and the eager looks from Idris, he would need to watch his back for a while.

Once his punishment was up, Kareem had gotten a note from Tejas to meet him in Falcon's Square tonight. It was named as such because of the giant falcon statue in the center of the fountain, looking as if it were midflight. As a child, Tejas used to dare Kareem to climb up there. The trick was to do it as fast as possible before nearby adults would come screeching in for him to get down.

The square was full of people this evening, enjoying the cooler air as the sun set and torches were lit. Kareem found Tejas sitting on a stone bench off to the side, popping seasoned nuts into his mouth one by one.

Ah! There's our troublemaker, he said as soon as he saw Kareem.

Kareem made an exasperated noise. Tejas couldn't even wait for him to say hello. *I didn't do anything,* he retorted. *Besides, I've already been punished, so there is no need to add to it.*

Tejas popped another nut into his mouth and glanced at him slyly. *If you didn't do anything, why were you punished?*

Kareem scowled as he sat down, realizing he had pigeonholed himself into that one.

So training isn't going well, Tejas surmised.

Kareem just grunted.

I see, Tejas said, watching the people in the square. This area of the city was slightly on the wealthier side but not like the homes near the central plaza or the northern quarter. It was still a nice area with the occasional orange, lemon, or mango tree planted in courtyards. There must have been several orange trees nearby because the air smelled sweet and citrusy.

I brought you something, Tejas said, as if just remembering. He pulled something shiny out of his pocket and dangled it before Kareem. It was a keychain with "Mykonos" written in bright colors. A little sunburst and blue wave were painted around the rim. He dropped it into Kareem's palm. It was something so foreign looking to Kareem despite having seen pictures of human cities and items, even after seeing them in markets here.

Great. You had a holiday in Greece while I was raking sand, Kareem said, flipping the plastic over in his hand. *How lucky of you.*

Tejas laughed lightly, but his face quicky turned serious. *It was no holiday.*

What happened? Kareem asked, pocketing the keychain.

Nothing, his brother said. There was a look on his face.

Did they find those missing citizens yet? The first wave people?

No.

I see. Kareem wondered what had happened to them. Could they have truly run out from under Rhapta's gaze?

Tejas turned to him. *Just be careful when you go on your first assignments. Okay?*

Okay.

Tejas grunted in approval, dropping the rest of the nuts into his mouth.

If I get arrested, I should give them a fake name, like Ignatius or something.

Well, no. You should avoid being arrested in the first place.

What if it can't be avoided?

Then you say nothing.

But they'd never let me go!

Kareem thought about how to explain that one. He and Ovi were lying on the roof, a spot he had found during his punishment. Kareem was lying on his back, squinting against the setting sun, trying to help Ovi with his human studies lessons. After Kareem had tackled Caden into the water, Ovi had been more open to talking to him. Kareem had also stayed away from pushing his teammates. He still wasn't ready to face what Laban—or Zara— had said to him, but he had managed to have some sort of basic friendship with Ovi. Despite being interested in ancient human medicine workers, Ovi had pitiful instincts when it came to the modern complexities of human society.

You have to try to find a way to escape, but saying anything would just make it worse. I would just do everything you can to avoid being caught, Kareem said.

Silence. *Will they experiment on me?* Ovi asked quietly.

Probably, Kareem replied bluntly. He swore he heard Ovi gulp. He had learned little things about him over the past few weeks, like how he didn't like soup and could name the properties of any plant he saw outside the walls of the city. Also, despite wanting to control his ability, Ovi had found excellent ways to avoid using it at all costs and was only forced to use it during abilities training. He told Kareem his test was similar to Idris's; he had to stun a beetle, but only enough not to kill it.

He hadn't succeeded yet.

Thankfully, if he accidentally touched a person, the effect wouldn't be a lot harder to recreate due to the size difference between human and beetle.

In contrast to the tentative friendship with Ovi, Zara had worked even harder to avoid Kareem. In their shared classes, she sat on opposite sides of the room and refused to even glance in his direction. In the hallways, she did the same, but Kareem hadn't failed to notice Faiza had started to give him a few appreciative glances despite her friend's cold shoulder toward him.

Kareem and Ovi heard a slight rustle and turned to see the door to the roof lift and Binita's head poking up. She had talked to them briefly a few times but never stayed long. The last time Kareem and Ovi had been studying, Binita had offered to give Kareem a few pointers to help him with his mental conditioning. She continued to excel in the class, and Kareem continued to avoid Laban's gaze like the sun avoids the moon.

Hi! Binita said as she came over to their spot. *Want to see my lizard?*

Kareem and Ovi glanced at each other. Binita, it had seemed, always had something odd; someone's hair comb, a bird's foot, a collection of mouse skulls, and now a lizard. It was small, only the length of her longest finger, but it scuttled inside her cupped hands.

That's cool, Binita, Ovi said, his voice straining. He gave her an honest smile.

How're human studies coming? she asked, tucking the lizard into the pocket of her uniform. How it stayed there, Kareem would never know.

Don't get arrested, only use verbal speech if needed, money comes in paper, metal, plastic, and electronic forms, and don't eat yellow snow, Ovi recited, looking down at his notes.

Hmph, sounds like it's going well, Binita said, sitting down beside them. She suddenly loomed over Kareem, wearing a different face. *And you? Have you progressed at all in your lack of mental control?* she said in Laban's voice.

Kareem gave an undignified yelp and swatted her away. *I'm working on it,* he grumbled.

Hey, she said, changing the subject, *have either of you heard that a few Anunnaki have gone missing? I mean the ones who went to live out in human society.*

Yeah, Ovi said, *Tarun mentioned it in class the other day when Tala wasn't in the room. They never checked in like they were supposed to, and none of the queen's advisers can locate them now.*

Kareem sat up. *I was just talking to my brother about this today. I think he's worried he might get taken too.*

Is your brother venari? Binita asked with a puzzled expression.

Yes, Kareem said. *His name is Tejas Maamoum. He's been venari for a long time.*

Oooh, Binita said, eyes widening. *I've seen him. He's cute!*

Kareem choked on whatever he was going to say.

Never seen him, Ovi said, a bit tersely.

Oh, you'd agree if you saw him, Binita said, nodding.

Anyway, Kareem said, punctuating each syllable, *Tejas has been out on assignments, and he won't say exactly, but I think he's worried about the missing Anunnaki. No one can find them, and the queen has several people with locator abilities in her employ.*

I wonder what happened to them, Ovi said quietly, twisting the hem of his uniform. They sat there in silence for a few moments. The city was quiet as well in the setting sun as if it was listening to their somber conversation. Kareem wondered what could have happened to those people. There wasn't enough justification for them to run away. They were allowed to live out in human society for the rest of their lives as decreed by the queen. What use was it to stop checking in and then disappear completely? Their first supervised assignment would be coming up soon, and apprehension sat appropriately in Kareem's mind. Tejas was right; he would need to be very careful.

I think they got abducted by aliens, Binita chirped, as if that was what they were all thinking.

Kareem and Ovi groaned in unison.

CHAPTER 9
SECRETS KEPT

*Y*ou *need to remember to blend in,* Afif, Kareem's human studies teacher was saying. He was a very short man with a voice to match, but his knowledge was as vast as the Sahara. *I suggest that you all practice speaking out loud before your assignments.*

I thought we weren't supposed to speak to humans, Samira said, raising her hand afterward.

You're not, Afif replied, holding a finger up. *But just in case.*

In case what? Tarun asked.

In case you have to speak, Afif said.

Why would we have to? Inaam asked now.

In case you want to buy something, Afif responded, confused by his own answer.

Like what?

Food.

Clothes?! Samira asked, perking up. Some of the students seemed excited at that.

Well, Afif said, a little flustered. *Yes, I suppose. All venari are allowed to keep human clothes so they can blend in.*

How much money do we get?

Afif sighed heavily.

It had been another week since Kareem, Ovi, and Binita had gathered on the roof, and it was almost time for their first supervised assignment. They would be going only in pairs with an experienced venari to hunt down a single ubir. It was really more like shadowing than anything. The venari would be doing most of the work while the pupils were meant to adjust to human society for the first time. Kareem was thrumming in both anticipation and worry. He had never left the city before, and it was both thrilling and terrifying. The assignment should be relatively easy, but you never knew what would happen. Kareem and Ovi would be going with Neelan, and Zara and Binita would go with another venari this time.

Across the room, Zara sat near the wall with her head down. Only occasionally would she talk to Inaam, who sat next to her, but never would she make eye contact with him. He had asked Binita about her, but the small girl only shrugged and said they had never talked.

All right, pupils, Afif said, *you are free to go early for the day. As a reminder, if you haven't already, you all need to have your tattoos adjusted before you go on your assignment tomorrow. Otherwise, the remainder of the day is for you to see your families before you go.*

Venari all received the additional, permanent ink to extend their Anunnaki tribe tattoos when they graduated, but pupils were only allowed the temporary ink until then. Kareem had gotten his during his break today. He had lain in an office upstairs while a venari he had never met had inked on additional whorls and designs around the tattoo in the center of his back. It stung at first, but quickly healed over, blending in with the tattoo he was born with. It would only last a week at most before he needed to be back in the city.

The pupils all got up to leave, and Kareem tried to catch Zara's eye as she walked out the door. Of course, she never even glanced his way. He had learned better than to try to follow her out into the hall. So he gathered his things and went on his own way, deciding to work on the issue that was Zara when he got back from his assignment. At the moment, he was more excited that he got to skip mental conditioning for a few days.

Mama, look what I made in school today, Akilah said, holding up a multilayered necklace of beads in every color.

Kareem huffed in frustration. He had been trying to tell his parents about his assignment tomorrow, but Akilah thought her schoolwork was more important than catching ubir.

We're listening, Kareem, his father said from behind his desk. It sat low on the ground near the big window, embroidered cushions underneath him as he wrote line after line of elegant script on the scroll that lay on his desk. He had looked up only once since Kareem had arrived nearly half an hour ago.

I was just saying that we are going to India tomorrow morning. My mentor told us a few days ago, Kareem said from his spot across the room. He felt he had a hard time sitting down right now, his feet wanting to pace back and forth in front of the tapestry that hung on the wall. His mother was cooing over Akilah's necklace, glancing at Kareem every now and again to show she was paying attention.

That's where the bears are, right? his father asked, still writing.

Well, there are bears—

Kareem, Akilah interjected, *did you make up with your girlfriend?*

Kareem blinked at her while his mother narrowed her eyes. *What girlfriend?* their father said, still writing.

I saw Kareem fighting with a girl a few weeks ago. She was mad, really mad. Akilah giggled and picked up her necklace again, twirling it around.

Kareem shook his head in annoyance. *She's not my girlfriend. She's my teammate. I'm the team leader, remember?*

Right, Akilah said with a snort that was beyond her years. Their parents had lost interest in the non-existent girlfriend.

Tejas was off somewhere, and Kareem had stopped home only to say goodbye to his parents. He didn't expect them to get mushy over him. They had come to terms with Tejas being on dangerous assignments years ago, so this barely rattled them. His mother had told him to be safe, and his father had given him a hearty *good luck* as if he were taking a test tomorrow. In a way, he was, he supposed.

India is a great country with vast amounts of... Kareem trailed off. His father was still writing, and his mother was looking at Akilah's other art projects from school. No one noticed when he stopped talking. After a few minutes of waiting, he stopped his pacing.

I have a few things I have to do before I leave tomorrow, so I need to get going.

His mother looked up then with a smile. *Remember to be safe.*

His father nodded in agreement, still writing. Akilah only noticed that the conversation had temporarily moved away for her, so she talked louder in their mother's ear, and Kareem bid his goodbye.

He closed the front door firmly on his way out. The sun was still in the sky since he had gotten off early, so the city was still active, many people still working. Kareem, in fact, did not have a single thing he needed to do before he left tomorrow. He had already been given a temporary set of human clothes and had packed a small bag that was also given to him. His room was tidy, his tattoo was fresh, and any schoolwork was already finished. If they needed anything else, Neelan would show them how to get it once they were in the human cities.

Kareem didn't want to go back to the house of the venari yet, so he wandered through the city instead. It had been well over a month since he had had the free time to do so during the day. Usually, he was only able to go out after his classes were done in the evening. The streets were busy as they normally were, and he found his way to one of the wide, baobab-lined boulevards headed south. He saw scholars, advisers, laborers, agriculturists with carts of food, warriors in their red paint with obsidian weapons, young children leaving school for the day, and even one or two venari. He passed by the shadow of the Grand Hall. He had never been inside and wondered if the queen actually lived there.

The streets were crowded, but they were rarely otherwise. His parents told him that Rhapta was much livelier than it had been even five years ago. The people who had lived in the outskirts of the city and the slums had moved into the south quarter that had been abandoned for decades, if not centuries. Being under the barrier had many health benefits for the Anunnaki that now lived there, strengthening their Auras, which helped heal them of human diseases and injuries. His mother had told him that meant more children were being born, much to the distress of Kareem's ears. A woman carrying two shrieking babies walked by, too close for comfort.

His walk took him around the Grand Hall, through the central plaza, down the boulevard, and into the southern quarter. If he kept going to the southern wall, he would find the quarries beyond —the vast pit where Aurastone was mined, the only one in the world. It was more chaotic here, with people packed in a little tighter. Instead of single-family homes, smaller homes were stacked on top of each other, connected only by a winding stone staircase outside. In the smaller courtyards, lines were connected across the streets, hung with clothes, flowers, or knickknacks.

Kareem passed by, kicking a small stone in front of him. A few people eyed his gray pupil's uniform, but none spoke to him directly. He turned down a street with small homes that had tiny courtyards in front of them, surrounded by low walls. Kareem immediately heard a woman's muffled sobbing. Just to his left, an old woman stood in the middle of one of those courtyards, clutching at a young girl, crying into her shoulder. The girl was murmuring soothing words in her ear. Something about the girl's hair struck Kareem...

The girl turned and caught him watching them, sending a shock through his system. He recognized her now.

It was Zara.

He didn't know why, but on instinct, he turned and ran back around the corner. Hopefully, she didn't recognize him as well.

His hopes were dashed when, seconds later, she came speed walking around the corner with an angry swing of her hair. She walked right up and immediately shoved him in the chest.

Why are you following me?! she screeched in his mind.

I-I'm not, Kareem got out. He was quite flabbergasted at the turn of events in his day. One minute he was taking a peaceful walk through the city; the next, he was accused of being a stalker. *I'm allowed to walk around the city freely,* he added. *I'm not a prisoner.*

Oh, and you just happened to be here? She placed her hands on her hips. Clearly, she was in the mood to fight.

Kareem, however, wasn't. *Well, yeah. What are you doing here?* he asked.

Zara went stiff. *That's none of your business.*

Kareem narrowed his eyes, looking over her shoulder. *Who was that woman anyway?*

Also none of your business. She stood there, still as a tree trunk and just as unmoving. She looked angrier than usual, and that was saying something. Her hands were balled into tight fists, and she was breathing heavily like she was expecting him to yell at her. Kareem was tired of fighting with her, though. It was possible that maybe, *maybe,* Zara had been partially correct. Maybe Kareem had been a little bossy at first. To be fair, he was just eager to become venari and wanted his team to do their best. And she hadn't been pleasant to deal with from the beginning. But he had spent weeks now trying to have a conversation to move forward. Would it always be like this? Her refusing to speak or even look at him?

One of Binita's tips for "godlike mental strength," as she called it, was to have harmony between your thoughts and your actions. To have full control of one's mind, you couldn't have any skeletons in the closet, fears pushed away unchecked, or avoided thoughts. She had told him to leave no stone left unturned in his mind. Avoiding things would make problems worse, not better. He had been trying not only to talk to Zara, but to at least peek under a few of the more unsavory stones in his mind. The ones that looked like conversations he had with Zara and Laban. He couldn't flip those stones entirely, but he had looked quickly before setting them back down.

So there was a small possibility that Kareem was partially to blame for the state of his relationship with his team.

Only a small possibility, though.

Kareem tugged at his collar. Rhapta was always hot, but the temperature had crept up over the last few seconds. After watching Zara fail at holding her ability for more than thirty seconds many times in class, Kareem knew he wouldn't have to wait long before the temperature dropped again.

They stood there, glaring at each other, Zara breathing hard but not moving. It looked like she wanted to say something, and Kareem found himself without words. It was probably for the best, though, as he always seemed to say the wrong thing around her.

A minute went by, and the temperature didn't drop. *Calm down, Zara,* Kareem muttered, flapping his shirt a little.

She's my mother, she blurted out angrily.

Kareem wondered if she meant the old woman, but that left Kareem confused. He had always assumed she was from a wealthy family due to the fact she had a servant bring her bags to the house on their first day. That and her haughty attitude. The house she and the woman were standing before was homely at best.

But the servant— he started.

That's none of your business! she snapped. She didn't move or run away, though, just kept standing there, glaring at him. The heat still hadn't broke, and he started to wonder if it was even her or just the sun. His back was sticky with sweat, and it started to bead on his forehead.

Well, I wasn't following you, he said, hoping that would appease her. He just didn't know what to *do* when it came to her. Anything he said angered her, but he felt like this was his only chance to talk to her before she gave him the cold shoulder again. It was always one or the other with her; boiling heat or frigid cold.

Why was she crying anyway? he asked warily.

As expected, her voice was dripping with acid. *Why do you think? I'm her only child. If I die, she will too.*

Kareem stared at her and felt like an idiot for not understanding her meaning. Why would her mother die if she died? Kareem stared at her and felt like an idiot for not understanding her meaning. Why would her mother die if she died? Why would Zara die at all? His expression must have shown his confusion because she let out a short, breathy laugh.

You are so spoiled, she said more to herself. *We are poor!* She was shouting now. *My mother is from the outskirts. She has a bad leg that can't be healed, so she can't work much. Any money has to come from me. If I die while out on an assignment, then she has no one to take care of her! Have you ever had to take care of anyone, Kareem?*

She was practically vomiting words now, and Kareem didn't stop her.

She has no one else, and this is the best option. Venari get paid well. Any money I make goes to her, but if I die, then she has nothing and will probably die of poverty as well. And I had to come and tell her that I'm leaving tomorrow. Which is why she was crying, you stupid buffoon.

She was really breathing hard now. The heat was still going, and it had been several minutes now.

Just don't pity me, she snarled before turning and running back the way she came, leaving Kareem standing perplexed in the middle of the street. Only when she was out of sight did the heat finally break.

Zara's abilities were getting better.

And she had *talked* to him.

Kareem smiled for the first time in a while.

CHAPTER 10

A FAR AWAY LAND

Kareem took several slow, deep breaths as he and Ovi followed Neelan across the field toward the edge of the forest. Far off to their right, Kareem could see a warrior with a spear slung across his back patrolling just beyond the tree line. There were many such guards along the edge of the barrier that demarked the perimeter of Rhapta. To humans that may pass by the outside, they would see nothing—not even the field Kareem walked across now. Since the threat to Rhapta caused by the former Elder Tahir five years ago, security around the city had been of the utmost importance. Kareem's own parents remembered seeing human machines—helicopters—flying over the unseen city, sending fear into every Rhaptan. They had come so close to being discovered back then.

And Kareem was about to leave.

The sun had not yet risen, but the sky was turning a bright shade of blue. New venari pupils would all be going out on supervised assignments as of today, albeit at different times and leaving in different directions. Kareem, Ovi, and Neelan were all dressed in dark human clothes. The fabric was heavier and more restrictive than he was used to, but Neelan said the pants and short-sleeved shirts would help them blend in.

Kareem yawned. He had stayed up later than he intended, thinking over his progress with Zara. He was almost giddy that she had talked to him, even if it was in the most threatening manner possible. He didn't plan on telling Ovi what he had learned of their teammate, not wanting to breach the fragile trust he had developed with Zara, if he could call it that.

They got to the edge of the forest and stepped into the trees. From his studies, Kareem remembered the barrier on the south side of the city was about fifty feet in, marked by a pole staked into the ground with feathers and beads attached to the top so none would miss it. He still couldn't believe he would be leaving the city. Even with the first wave of people testing relocation into human cities, most Rhaptans never left the city and never would. Anticipation thrummed in Kareem's veins. He tried to remember every detail about human civilization as he could as they made their way to its edge.

The barrier is up here, Neelan said, adjusting the bag sitting on his back. *It feels a bit odd going through, but it's nothing, really.*

Kareem and Ovi glanced at each other. Ovi was wearing a pair of thin black gloves in addition to his human clothes. Kareem knew he was more nervous than him about going out into human society. His ability was still something he feared despite Kareem having never seen him use it.

The pole came into view, and Neelan didn't hesitate as he stepped beyond it. Nothing changed as he kept walking. Was the barrier there or further into the trees? Kareem and Ovi followed, the former holding his breath as he walked by the pole.

It felt like a faint tugging, as if he had walked into a thick cobweb. He stepped beyond the pole and...

Nothing. He felt no different. He looked to Ovi, who had stopped beside him, eyes wide.

Is that it? Ovi asked, looking around. The trees were the same; the lightening sky was still there. They felt no different.

I guess so, Kareem said, almost disappointed that he didn't feel grander.

"From here on out, we talk out loud," Neelan said, the sound startling them. It sounded weird and far away to Kareem's mind, even though Neelan was right in front of them. Not that no one *ever* spoke out loud in Rhapta, but it was so uncommon, and Kareem hadn't been expecting it.

"Okay," he said tentatively. His voice felt rough and unused. It sounded the same as the one he had in his head. Ovi just nodded.

Neelan turned and started heading through the trees at a brisk pace. "It will take several hours to get to Moshi—the nearest town with a portal. From there, we go to Jaipur. I intend to be there and settled before the afternoon, and the trek down the hill is the worst part, so let's get going."

Kareem followed Neelan through the forest, which started to slope downward quickly. He was still too excited to pay much attention to the area around them and the incessant mosquitos that bit at his face and arms. Knots of anticipation had started forming in his stomach from the time he woke up. He would see humans today! And travel to the other side of the planet. The thought was mind-boggling in itself, and he relished the pride he felt at getting to do so.

The next time they saw anything, Kareem was soaked with sweat, and his feet hurt from walking so much, but Neelan turned to face them. "The highway is just up ahead. Moshi isn't far, so we'll walk, but I sometimes try to catch a ride or a bus if we see one. Keep your eyes open."

Kareem and Ovi walked faster and came to the road just after Neelan. It was odd seeing a large strip of pavement that wasn't built from the white limestone like in Rhapta. Neelan suddenly stopped.

"Oh, I forgot," he said, pulling his bag off and unzipping it. "I need to give you two these." He handed each of them a stack of small plastic cards, and Kareem was surprised to see a perfect replica of his face on his. "IDs," Neelan explained, "which you should have learned about in your classes already. These are very important if you ever need to 'prove' your identity. I've given you ones for a few different countries, so don't get caught with the whole stack. That would be suspicious. Just try not to get caught in the first place."

Ovi was flipping through each one, looking over the details. Kareem pocketed his and nodded. Satisfied now, Neelan threw his bag back across his shoulder and turned down the road. They started walking along, and a humming had Kareem glancing back up the road. His intake of breath came a millisecond before the vehicle zipped by. It was a small sedan and was gone before Kareem got a chance to really see it.

"Was that a car?" Ovi said, his voice scratchy. "It was going so *fast*. They're going to get hurt!"

Neelan chuckled. "Yeah, that was a car. Get used to them."

The three of them kept walking, and Kareem and Ovi marveled whenever one of them flew by, noting their different shapes and colors. They had seen pictures before, but nothing prepared them for the sheer speed they moved at. A bus finally came down the road and seemed to slow for them, Neelan waving at the driver.

"Okay, we're getting on. I'll pay for both of you, just remember the rules," Neelan quickly said as they jogged up to the door and climbed up the steps. Kareem's heart was pounding as he followed Neelan onto the bus. People—humans!—glanced at him as they made their way to the back. There was too much to look at, and Kareem and Ovi were both breathing fast as they sat down. Some of the people were talking, and some sort of music was coming from somewhere, but he couldn't see where. Kareem mentally played over the rules he had to follow in his head while trying to remember what languages were spoken in what areas of the world.

Neelan let out a single laugh when he saw Kareem and Ovi's stricken faces as the bus pulled back onto the road and sped off. Kareem gripped the seat in front of him for dear life, making the lady in front of him turn him a glare. The next forty-five minutes passed by in an overstimulated blur. Kareem and Ovi bounced on the bus that moved too fast, then pulled off at a stop indicated by Neelan into the heart of a bustling city. The sheer noise of spoken speech had his ears ringing, and there was so much to take in he wasn't sure if the sweat dripping down his face was from the heat or anxiety. He and Ovi unconsciously stuck together as Neelan led them through throngs of people like a fish through weeds.

They came to a small house in a quieter neighborhood, and Neelan knocked on the door. They were let inside by an exasperated woman speaking in the local language. She had two young children playing around her legs and alternated between yelling at them and admonishing Neelan. Kareem had studied many languages and picked up bits and pieces and was now deciphering the unpleasant words she was directing at Neelan. He introduced them to her as Bahati, the Ummanu who guarded the portal here. She glanced at them with only slightly less hostility than she did at the cackling children that swarmed her legs.

Bahati led them into another room in her house that was used for the portal. While she bustled into the other room to chase off the children, Kareem said to Neelan, *Is she always so displeased with you?*

Every time, came his sigh into Kareem's mind.

The room they were in was devoid of anything except for a few crystals piled into the corner. Bahati came back with an armload more. After confirming with Neelan where they wanted to go, she got to work setting up a line of crystals on the floor in an order that Kareem couldn't distinguish. Kareem knew when she placed the last one because a rippling wave of energy rose like steam suddenly. He sucked in a breath, trying to get his eyes to understand what he was seeing. Despite having been around Anunnaki abilities all his life, Kareem was in awe of the thing before him. How was it that this shimmering mirage that undulated above the crystals would allow them to travel *across the planet?*

He knew venari traveled this way every day, but it was hard for even him to wrap his mind around it. Bahati was standing to the side with an expression that said she didn't have all day. Neelan looked at him and Ovi. "The best way to do this is to just go for it. I'll see you on the other side."

"Wait—" Ovi started to say, but Neelan was already walking through. It looked like he was about to run into the wall on the other side, but his form vanished *into* the rippling air.

Kareem and Ovi didn't have time to marvel because Bahati was looking ready to shove them through. Kareem clenched his jaw and strode forward with a surety that he would run smack into the wall. His heart stuttered just before he did, and he felt suddenly cold all over as he stepped into the portal. A different kind of heat accosted him then, and Kareem knew he had made it.

A retching sound came from his right, and he looked around to find Ovi vomiting on the floor beside him. They were in another house, but he couldn't see much beyond the room he was in. The air smelled different here as well. Neelan was on the other side of the small room, apologizing to a man who smiled and shook his head. An older man sat on a stool near the doorway, nodded, and smiled at Kareem like he had just won a grand prize before taking a sip out of a mug. He laughed with delight when Ovi stood upright again, looking miserable.

Kareem and Ovi were soon again rushed through the house without getting time to absorb everything that they had been experiencing over the last hour. Kareem's mind was reeling that he was somehow supposed to be in India now. He didn't believe it until his breath caught when he passed by an open balcony.

A city rivaling the size of Rhapta sprawled out in the valleys between several hills, stretching down into the plains that looked south based on the sun's position. The house they were in must have been on the side of one such hill, and Kareem saw a myriad of homes, complexes, and what looked like palaces that looked more magnificent than the Great Hall. The serenity of the scene left his mind blank. Kareem couldn't deny that he had been transported across the world and was staring down at one of the humans' most glorious cities: Jaipur.

Heeding Neelan's insistence, Kareem pulled himself from the view and followed him and Ovi down into the heart of the city.

CHAOS. Absolute chaos was how Kareem would describe the streets of Jaipur. He wanted to laugh at himself for thinking Moshi was busy. The idea that the small town in Tanzania they had come from was overstimulating to his nerves was fallacious at best and downright comical at its worst.

The first thing Kareem discovered were the bikes. Both the pedal and motorized variety. They were everywhere he looked, moving at jarring speeds and with seemingly no pattern or recognition of law. That, coupled with the massive number of people somehow talking simultaneously, left him practically dizzy as he focused on keeping Neelan's back in front of him. Ovi had more than once run face-first into Kareem, giving him the impression the other boy was just as disoriented. There were bright colors everywhere he looked, from signs to goods to clothing. Quite a fair amount of the buildings were painted the same faded salmon color that had him confused about which way they were going and where they had come from. Despite the city accosting every one of his senses, it was just as magnificent from the ground as it was from up on the hill—just with a different perspective.

Neelan was leading them to check into a motel. As they walked, Neelan told them the plan was to stay the night, attempt to capture the ubir tomorrow, and head straight back to Rhapta. After they checked in, they would spend the afternoon scavenging the city for the ubir to get an idea of their location. Kareem knew Neelan was trying to keep them from feeling too overwhelmed, but he kept finding himself staring at the motorbikes that zipped past and between the cars. It couldn't be that hard...

"Don't even think about it." Neelan had turned a bright green eye on him in a way that made him feel foolish. "The locals have a particular skill set in driving in these conditions. That or a death wish," he added under his breath. Kareem was inclined to agree. More than once had he strayed too far into the street only to be honked at as a motorbike swerved around him.

"The ubir's name is Aamadu," he continued. "He's supposedly an older man with his tattoo on his neck, so he should be easy to spot."

"What's his ability?" Ovi asked, walking quickly to keep up.

"We don't know," Neelan said. "Any information we get is from the seers, so it comes in fragments. That means we know little and need to work quickly. And *be careful.* Remember, you are only shadowing me on this assignment. I will do all the work, and you will not participate." He turned to look at them. "Is that understood? This is very important."

They both nodded, Kareem trying to keep his focus when those bikes kept speeding past. How powerful he would feel with the wind gliding over his head...

They checked in at the motel Neelan steered them to, a large building broken into many smaller rooms that were rented out. The staff was generous and eager to show them inside. Neelan spoke to them for a few minutes, and then they were back out on the bustling streets.

"Let's go take a look around the city and see what information we can find," Neelan said, wiping his brow and taking a drink from a bottle of water. "It would be nice to be done tomorrow, but you never know. It could take days to find him." He shrugged and slipped the bottle into his bag.

Kareem followed him back through winding streets, past markets that looked strikingly similar to those in Rhapta, and around the perimeter of buildings big enough to be palaces. Maybe they were. Ovi stayed close to the two of them, keeping his gloved hands tight to himself. He had opted for long sleeves and pants despite the heat.

"Ovi, how is the training with your ability coming along?" Neelan asked, eyeing the younger boy. "Are you able to paralyze others without hurting them yet?"

"No," Ovi said sourly. "I've been practicing on beetles, but not yet. They always die."

"Don't worry," Neelan said brightly. "It'll take time. Let's just not test it today," he added with a nervous chuckle.

They walked the streets of Jaipur and through a neighborhood that had a late afternoon lull. The area curved up toward the city's surrounding hills, the sun glancing over the top and casting long shadows between the homes on this side. Kareem was wide awake, though, remembering the time difference from traveling halfway around the world in such a short period of time. He was thrumming with energy again, wanting to see and learn everything. He wanted to experience the life the humans had and all of the things they clung to.

Neelan had stopped to ask a few people some questions. Kareem and Ovi were listening in, trying to get an idea of how Neelan spoke to them without giving away they were Anunnaki. The locals didn't seem overly eager to talk and shook their heads, waving as they walked away. Neelan tried again with a few men down the street, and a few more after that. He finally came back and nodded toward a smaller side street to their right.

"None of them would tell me anything outright, but I got the impression something happened a few streets up here the last few nights. Something about a loud sound they heard and maybe a scream. Apparently, no one wants to investigate those things here," Neelan muttered. "If you didn't see it, it didn't happen." He sighed.

They followed Neelan down the street, glancing left and right at the little alleys that broke off in between homes and buildings in either direction. The further they went, the more the street started to slope up gently. It was much quieter in this area, with deep shadows that would linger day and night.

If the ubir was still around, he would be here.

Neelan seemed to sense this as well and started to tense up, every movement deliberate as he glanced down the alleys. He paused, peering down at one of them more intently.

"Wait here," he said. He tilted his head down slightly to better look them in the eyes. "Remember, under no circumstances are you to interfere. If it looks dangerous, turn and run. I'll find you later."

Both of them nodded, still looking around, waiting for some sort of monster to emerge from the alley. In contrast, the middle of the street was still bright and sunny, giving an eerie quality to the area. Neelan slung his bag tighter across his back but not before slipping a small, obsidian dagger from one of the pockets, palming it in his hand. He went into the alley on the right, disappearing down its corridors.

Once he was gone, Kareem's nerves shot up. What if the ubir came when he was gone? They had been training for over a month now, and he felt he and Ovi both had learned much in that time. The prospect of seeing—and capturing—an ubir had his eyes wide as he kept a lookout.

They waited for Neelan but heard nothing. The minutes crept by, and a few people passed them, but the street remained mostly empty here. It took a moment for the awareness to kick in, but goosebumps spread over Kareem's arms, and his spine stiffened.

They were being watched.

Ovi seemed to sense it, too, his breath coming fast next to Kareem as they stood close to each other. Kareem looked around. Nothing stood out to him from where he stood until—there, the alley to his left was empty save for a few boxes and discarded trash, more shadows lingering further down where the alley split off into separate directions.

There among the shadows, half-hidden by the low building, stood a man. His eyes were wide open, too wide to be considered normal. His mouth was open as well, panting. He stared at them, unmoving. Kareem was momentarily frozen in fear at the horrific, animalistic expression on the man's face. It made his legs weak and his stomach cramp. The clouds above passed over the sun, shifting the shadows in the alley, allowing Kareem to get a better look at their watcher.

A red welt on his neck looked like a twisted wound. Kareem squinted. It looked almost like...

The mark of the Anunnaki.

The ubir must have noticed Kareem's change in expression because he turned and ran into one of the branching alleys.

"It's him!" Kareem shouted, and a thrill took over him at seeing the ubir flee. His own legs were suddenly moving, sprinting down the alley after him. He didn't pay attention to Ovi's shouts to stop. All Kareem saw was the ubir getting away. He followed him into the twists and turns of the alleys between the neighborhoods, bouncing in and out of shafts of light from above and back into the darkness of the shadows. He was faintly aware of footsteps behind him but focused on the tufts of gray hair sticking out of the ubir's head and his ratty clothes.

It started to feel like they were going in circles, and Kareem was delighted when the ubir took a familiar turn. Kareem took a sooner turn to cut him off on the other side of the low building.

Just as suspected, the ubir's garbled cry of anger came when Kareem barreled into him by surprise. They both slammed into the side of the building, and Kareem blindly fumbled for any part of the ubir he could get ahold of. Somehow in the mess of limbs, he managed to *stick* the ubir's arm to the wall and shot back out of reach.

He was gasping for breath but smiling when he saw the ubir, eyes crazed, realizing his arm was fully attached to the wall. It would be several minutes before it would release, in time for Neelan to arrive.

He had done it!

Ovi came panting around the corner to a halt, eyes widening at the ubir struggling to remove his arm.

"What did you do?" Ovi whispered, inching closer. His expression was mixed with both shock and horror at seeing an ubir for the first time. The ubir bellowed in anger as Ovi advanced toward them.

"I caught him!" Kareem said, still smiling as he tried to catch his breath. "We just have to get Neelan—"

The ubir snarled in reply, wrenching his arm away from the wall this time—hard. Doubt quickly turned into an avalanche of fear as an entire section of wall broke away, still stuck to the ubir's arm. Kareem and Ovi gaped as pieces of cinder block crumbled off the ubir's arm, even as he swung the entire rocky thing into Ovi. The breath rushed out of the boy's chest, and he flew back, his head making a sickening crack against the opposite wall.

Kareem looked at Ovi, unmoving on the ground, and then at the enraged ubir who stood like some half-Anunnaki half-concrete monster before him.

What had he done?

The ubir took a single step before something small and dark rocketed through the alley, lodging hard in the ubir's stomach. The cries of rage turned into yelps of angered pain.

Neelan stood at the mouth of the alley, looking nearly as angry as the ubir with something like a twinge of fear. He glanced down at the unmoving boy, but the ubir had turned to run down the alley. On instinct, Kareem turned toward him, taking steps to follow.

"*Don't!*" Neelan hissed, the tone sending a shock of shame through Kareem. "We need to get Ovi out of here." He picked up the boy and slung him over his shoulder like a sack of flour. "Let's go."

Kareem numbly followed, letting the ubir disappear the other way.

CHAPTER II
REPERCUSSIONS

Kareem sat on one of the three small beds shoved inside the modest-sized motel room. Ovi lay on one of the others while Neelan cleaned his wounds. Blood had poured like a river from a gash behind his right ear. The flow had stopped, but Ovi was still unconscious. Anunnaki healed much faster than humans and were harder to kill because of it, but they were not immortal. The outer wound may have sealed already, but it was possible he still had internal bleeding.

A vise of guilt gripped Kareem, making it hard to sit still on the bed. He twisted his fingers and tapped his legs. Neelan had said nothing to him on the rush back to the motel. It had darkened by the time they got there, Neelan carrying Ovi in like a drunk relative, a grossly underage one.

"He needs a healer," Neelan mumbled, wiping away some of the blood to peer at the boy. The look of absolute disappointment he had given Kareem in the alley would haunt him for weeks, if not the rest of his life. He jerked his chin to the corner where a small table was filled with paper cups and tea bags. "Make him some tea. I think he'll wake soon."

Obediently, Kareem did as he was told, heating the water and ripping open the tin sachet. He glanced back to the bed where his roommate and possibly friend lay unmoving, save for the rapid rise and fall of his chest. What if he died? How would Kareem live with himself? He focused on pouring the water to keep his hands from shaking. By the time he turned back, Neelan had stopped and was assessing him now with those green eyes, his face devoid of expression.

Kareem waited for the scathing words to come, the reprimand, the expulsion from the house of the venari. He wouldn't be surprised if he was locked in the dungeons deep beneath Rhapta. Neelan shook his head suddenly, as if having decided something, and sighed. Kareem set the tea on one of the bedside tables.

"I'll be back in a little while," Neelan said, standing to retrieve his bag. "You are not to leave," he said calmly. "Try to get some sleep. We are leaving as soon as I return." The door clicked shut before Kareem could open his mouth. Neelan's reaction, or lack thereof, couldn't have hurt worse.

Tears welled in Kareem's eyes as he sat on one of the beds and waited for Ovi to wake.

THE HOURS TICKED BY. Kareem dozed in a fit of anxiety, woken only when he heard Ovi's sudden intake of breath. The other boy groaned, and Kareem shot to his feet.

"Ow," Ovi said, bringing a hand to his head as he tried to sit up. Kareem rushed over and handed him the cold tea.

"Ovi, I am *so* sorry—"

"Mmhmm," Ovi hummed as he gulped down the liquid.

"If I had known what was going to"—Kareem took a breath—"I mean, I had no idea that—"

"It's fine," Ovi got out, handing back the cup and sinking into the pillows. The gash had fully healed, but his breaths were shallow, and he looked beyond tired. "I was actually kind of impressed," he said, closing his eyes.

"W-what?" Kareem stuttered.

"Yeah," Ovi said, eyes still closed. "You actually managed to trap an ubir on our first time. That's crazy." He gave a little smile. "That ubir must've had a strengsh abilly ta rip the wall. That sticky stuff of yers relly does come in andy dou…" Ovi's words were starting to slur together, and his head fell to the side. Kareem waited to see if he would say more, but he had fallen asleep.

Kareem wanted to shake him awake and apologize until his face turned blue. Ovi's condition wasn't improving fast enough. What if he had brain damage? Or died of a fever? Kareem wanted to wail in frustration and self-hatred. He settled with sitting back on the other bed, and soon he fell asleep too.

A BANG RIPPED Kareem from his nightmare of dark alleys and wide, staring eyes. Neelan strode into the room, turning on the lights.

"Let's go," he said. It looked like he had aged years since he left. Dark circles hung under his eyes, and his shoulders slumped with weariness. Was this the same man who had played the mbira in his room just a few weeks ago? Shame came barreling back into Kareem that he had such an effect on his mentor.

Neelan was throwing their few items into bags. There was dried blood on his shoulder, and his shirt was torn at the side. Kareem was too afraid to ask and just helped Ovi up. He woke but mumbled complaints until Neelan promised to get him to a healer as soon as possible.

They were out the door in less than two minutes, Neelan carrying Ovi out and Kareem with the bags. In the small lobby, the desk sat empty at this late hour. The clock on the wall indicated it was two o'clock in the morning, but Kareem felt as if he were missing chunks of time. He followed Neelan out to the curb and into a waiting cab that sped them across the city. He couldn't even enjoy the ride for all the misery he felt at seeing Ovi slumped, half-asleep next to him.

They moved at dizzying speeds and soon found themselves in front of the Ummanu's house again. Neelan paid the driver and grabbed Ovi again, carrying him up the steps. The door was open, and the old man sat on his stood, puffing on a pipe, his face contemplative this time as the three of them hurried inside. The other man was waiting for them in the hall and turned to lead them back into the house to a far room. Neelan left Ovi with Kareem and went inside, nodding to a woman around Kareem's mother's age who stood outside the door.

Kareem's heart stuttered, and he flattened against the wall with Ovi in tow when Neelan emerged, hauling the ubir out in front of him. The wild-eyed ubir—Aamadu—looked almost drugged now, bound in lengths of a silvery rope. Laqueus bound an Anunnaki's abilities but also caused them pain in doing so. Hessa had forced them to test it out on each other weeks ago, and Kareem wasn't eager to do it again anytime soon.

Neelan shoved the ubir into the room with the portal just down the hall. He spoke a few words to the man, and they opened the portal in a similar way Bahati had. There was no time for good-byes as the rippling air emerged, and the four of them went through. Bahati herself was just rushing into the room on the other side. How she knew they were coming, Kareem didn't know. By the sound of her immediate string of curses at Neelan, she didn't appreciate being woken at that hour. Neelan calmed her down and somehow got her to allow them to wait in another room of her house while Neelan left to get a car.

That left Kareem alone with a half-conscious Ovi and the ubir. They sat in the half-dark with only the hallway light on. When

Kareem had seen the ubir the first time, he had been frightened at his demeanor but had quickly realized he was just another person —one without venari training—and Kareem had felt more confident. But Kareem had quickly seen what such a person was capable of.

The ubir didn't try to speak, just glared at Kareem with bloodshot eyes, spittle coming out with his heavy breaths. Kareem didn't dare take his eyes away from him until Neelan came back ten minutes later. They went outside to find a car waiting, and Kareem didn't bother asking where he got it from. The ubir was shoved in the trunk as Kareem helped Ovi into the back.

The ride back to the mountain took half the time it did on the bus. Neelan must have been going well over the speed limit to make it that fast. He pulled off to the side of the road by the woods that coated Mount Kilimanjaro and cut the engine.

The next few hours were some of the most miserable of Kareem's life. They normally wouldn't have bothered trying to make it up the mountain in the dark, but Neelan had insisted Ovi needed a healer and handed Kareem a heavy flashlight. Neelan kept the ubir in front of him, and Kareem helped a stumbling Ovi through the trees. For some reason, the darkness stretched Kareem's guilt wide open. He panted and sweat in the night heat, feeling pathetic. He could only blame himself for the situation they were in. The training sessions with Hessa were nothing like trying to hike up a mountain, in the dark, with an injured friend and a bound ubir while tripping every two seconds. His mind eventually went blank as he focused on just making it up there alive. He had to carry Ovi on his back part of the way up as Neelan couldn't do anything but focus on the ubir.

When they got to the pole staked into the ground the demarked the city limit, Kareem could have wept. The rest of the way through the barrier to the city was nothing in comparison. They hurried into Rhapta's walls, Neelan leading them a back way to avoid running through the city proper with an ubir. He took them to a small building not far from the house of the venari. Kareem was deliriously tired at this point, Ovi hanging off him and burning up from a fever. Inside the small building was a single door, surprisingly guarded by two warriors.

Stay here, Neelan said and dragged the ubir toward the door. The two warriors nodded to him and opened it. A staircase led down, and that's all Kareem saw until the warriors closed the door. Minutes later, Neelan came back up without the ubir this time. He picked Ovi up and led them back to the house of the venari. It was dark and quiet inside, the venari and pupils sleeping at this hour, only a few on watch. Neelan took the stairs by the door to the second level, heading straight for Savar's office. The light was on beneath the door. What was Savar doing up at this hour?

Neelan only had to knock once before Savar yanked the door open with a stony expression. He took one look at Ovi and ushered them inside, having Neelan lay Ovi on a cot in the corner of the room. He was awake but barely, sweat pouring down his face. Another unknown venari was in the room with Savar, and he sent him to fetch a healer. The man was out in an instant.

Neelan then told Savar what happened, sparing none of the details as Kareem stood awkwardly in the doorway, feeling his shame all over again. Savar glanced at Kareem a few times, frowning but not otherwise giving anything away. The healer came, and Kareem sagged in relief when her first words were that Ovi would be just fine.

He wouldn't die.

Neelan and Savar continued to speak, but Kareem was dead on his feet, eyelids drooping as his head lolled to the doorframe. He picked up the end of the conversation.

I don't like to do this, Savar said, *but I have another assignment for you. You leave in the morning.*

Neelan's brows furrowed. *Can't someone else go? That's only a few hours from now.*

We are short on venari. Most are out with the pupils at the moment. You are the first ones back, Savar said. *This can't wait. Someone has to look into it now, and the queen won't let me send Zaid.* He practically growled the last few words.

Neelan sighed. *Okay, just give me the details.*

Savar nodded. *They'll be ready for you when you leave.* He glanced at Kareem by the door. *Your team will be looked after until you get back, but it shouldn't take long.*

Neelan seemed to have just remembered Kareem was still there and came over to him. *Go back to your room for the night.* He seemed far more tired than Kareem felt.

But what about my punishment—

Neelan shook his head. *Just go.*

On heavy feet, Kareem slipped from the doorway and found his way through the dark.

CHAPTER 12

THE HOPE OF PROGRESS

Kareem trudged down the stairs to the training pit, ignoring the calls of his bed. He could just make out the lightening blue of the sky above the ring, but the air was cooler this morning. Gray-uniformed pupils gathered in the sand, waiting for the others and Hessa to arrive. It had been two days since the mad dash back to the city, and Kareem was still processing the whirlwind events.

He spotted Ovi sitting in the sand with Binita and Zara, surprisingly, across from him. As he got closer, he heard Binita's rapid-fire recount of her and Zara's assignment.

There were lights in the sky! she said, twirling her arms above her head. *I have never been so cold in my life. Minus when Zara's in a bad mood,* she added. The girl in question just rolled her eyes. *It took Baava less than two days to capture the ubir. The lunatic was hiding in someone's sauna!* She laughed.

And you just got back last night? Ovi asked. *Aren't you tired?*

Yes, we are very tired, Zara insisted. Upon seeing Kareem stride over, she turned him a hostile glare.

Back to normal, then.

We heard what happened, Binita said, glancing at both Ovi and Kareem, who stood at the edge of your circle. *Glad you didn't die or anything. That would've sucked.*

Zara snorted, but Ovi said, *Yeah, I'm fine. This one is the worst sort of mother hen,* he said, jerking a thumb in Kareem's direction.

After Ovi had woken fully the day prior, Kareem had spent a copious amount of time apologizing again before taking every opportunity to make sure he was all right and didn't need anything. At one point, Ovi threatened to kick him out of the room if he didn't stop apologizing.

He had been in his own sort of misery as well. Savar finally called him into his office the night before after no word for two days. Kareem had walked to his office like he would his funeral, and for the second time, he sat before the leader of the venari for hurting someone. This time had been a thousand times worse than the first.

Do you know why you are here? Savar had asked.

Kareem had nodded, staring at his lap. His cuticles were scraped away from the constant wringing and picking at his fingers.

Do you know what you did wrong?

Kareem nodded again. When the older venari didn't respond, Kareem looked up to find him studying him.

I am fond of natural consequences, he said. *I assume you have been wallowing in your own misery these last few days?*

That was an understatement. *Yes, sir.*

It's ironic, Savar mused, leaning back. *The last time you were sitting in that spot was for defending the boy that you have now gotten hurt.*

Kareem's shoulders were hunched.

You have a good friend in that one, Savar added. *The first thing he said when he woke was how 'cool' you were to have trapped an ubir on your first try.*

Ovi must have hit his head harder than Kareem had thought.

Savar sighed. *You do look pathetic, and you are torturing yourself far more than I ever could. I won't be expelling you. Just make sure you don't lose those friends you have.*

KAREEM HAD REALIZED Savar was right; Ovi *was* his friend. And looking at Binita and Zara gathered around him, maybe they could be his friends too. The thought of any of them getting hurt, even Zara, had him wanting to throw up in the sand.

Hessa's voice broke him from his wallowing, calling all pupils to do two laps around the city.

She is crazy, Zara fumed as she got to her feet. *A kid almost died, and she wants us running double laps?*

Kareem almost enjoyed the physical punishment to his legs and lungs this morning. He went through the routine that had slowly become a familiar and steady presence in his life over the last weeks. It was a safe routine. Nothing bad was going to happen, like having your friend hurtled into a wall by a crazed monster. When they finished their warm-ups, Hessa gave them barely enough time to catch their breath before she called them to form two parallel lines for sparring. Kareem was paired with Veer.

Can we use our abilities? Caden asked.

Hessa strolled around the ring while they got into place, hands clasped behind her back. *No,* she said firmly, glancing at the slight shake of his head.

They were each supposed to do three rounds with their opponent before Hessa would call for them to switch. Kareem and Veer were a good match. Both were on the bulkier side, but Kareem matched his speed to Veer's strength. Wooden practice swords clashed and bruised each other's knuckles. They each won a round, with Kareem narrowly winning the third.

Everyone, take a step to your left, and you will find your new opponent, Hessa called to the group. Kareem found himself standing before Zara.

Great.

They hadn't talked since their fight outside her house when she told him about her mother's situation. It had been more than she had ever told him about herself, but that didn't seem to make a difference now. She stood across from him, two wooden daggers in her hands. Kareem dropped his short sword to match her daggers.

The first round was a mess. They stumbled and lurched, each circling the other, barely getting in hits on each other. It ended when Kareem started to charge her, and she reeled back, tripping and falling into the sand.

That only made her angry.

The second round was no better. She crouched low, feigning left and right. Her gaze was hostile, but she was watching him, waiting for him to make a move.

Kareem stood upright. He understood then that she was actually waiting for him to make a move.

You give in? she asked, fists on hips, still with the daggers.

Kareem shook his head, walked over to her, and pretended to show her his dagger, not that the sparring pupils were paying them any mind. *I didn't tell Ovi or anyone else about the thing with your mom.*

She looked at him warily. *Good, you were being nosy. It's none of your business anyway.* She crossed her arms.

Kareem exhaled a breath and looked dead into her icy eyes. *I just wanted you to know that yes, it's none of my business, so I don't plan on telling anyone else. You can tell them if you want or not. I just want us to focus on our training so no one gets hurt when we go on assignments.*

You mean like how you hurt Ovi? she tossed back at him.

Yes, exactly like that, he said. She narrowed her eyes at his agreement. *I don't care what you do outside of training, but I just want us to at least practice while we are here so that doesn't happen in the future. That's all. Okay?*

She looked him over, her gaze distrusting, but she gave a tiny, firm nod. *Fine*, she said lightly. *Switch to short swords.*

Kareem backed up and dropped his daggers, coming back with the sword. They continued their sparring, and Zara kept her eyes focused on his movements this time. She was very different with a sword, he quickly realized. Her movements were elegant with a deadly finish.

She won the second two times, but Kareem felt like he was the one who had won.

THE REST of the day passed better than expected. There seemed to be a shift in the dynamics of Kareem's team. Binita sat next to him for once in their mental conditioning class, and Zara even glanced at him in their abilities training class. It was a marginal change at best, but he would take it.

By the time evening came, Kareem and Ovi were up on the roof again, enjoying the breeze as they worked on material from their classes. Despite nearly dying on their first assignment, Ovi jumped back into his studies with vigor. Both he and Kareem found they had mountains of questions after having experienced human life for the first time. It was one thing reading about it and another living it.

The door to the roof creaked open, and Binita scrambled up with a stack of papers wedged under her arm. To Kareem's surprise, Zara was right behind her.

Here are my recommendations, Binita said, coming over. She handed Kareem the stack of papers with barely legible scrawl. *You need exercises to help your mental focus. These should help.*

Kareem glanced over the list of items like 'stare a gecko in his left eye for a turn of the hour' and 'stand in the middle of the central plaza without moving for traffic.'

Thanks, Binita, he said. *Are you staying to study?* He glanced at Zara, but she was looking off into the distance.

No, Binita replied, *we are going to go spar in a field or something. See you tomorrow!*

She turned to leave, but Kareem found himself saying, *Wait! While we're all here—*

Zara let out an exasperated sigh.

—I have something to say. Kareem took a breath and looked at the three of them. *I just want to say sorry for being a jerk.*

They all blinked at him in unison.

I told Zara this earlier, he continued, squaring his shoulders, *but I really want our team to be focused on our training together. I know we've had a bit of a rocky beginning, but I don't want anyone else to get hurt the way Ovi got hurt. I mean, he seriously could've—*

Ovi groaned, tilting his head back. *You're not going to get mushy again, are you? I told you I'm fine.*

I'm not, I'm not, Kareem said, putting his hands up amid Binita's laughter. *Can we all just agree to work on our classes a little so we can avoid dying on our assignments? The next skirmish is coming up soon, and if we happen to win, we'll be going on our first assignment alone. Neelan and the other mentors won't be there. Can we at least agree on that?*

Ovi nods, as does Binita slowly. Even Zara nodded.

Speaking of, Binita said, *where is Neelan? I haven't seen him since we got back.*

Savar sent him on another assignment right after we got back, Kareem said. *He should be back soon, though. How about we plan to meet here a few times a week?* he asked, getting back to the topic at hand.

Ovi and Binita agreed again. Kareem chanced another look at Zara. She didn't immediately bite his head off and bobbed her chin in something of a nod. He would take that as a yes.

Great, let's get back to work then.

CHAPTER 13

THE RISE OF FEAR

*Y*ou *need to relax,* Kareem said louder. *Thrashing will only make you sink faster.*

I don't want to sink at all! Ovi shouted, throwing his arms around in a manner that made him look like he was trying to fly instead of swim.

You won't, Kareem replied. *The stream is shallow, you can just stand up.*

They were in the woods near the stream where Kareem used to do his morning exercises before becoming a venari pupil. He stood on the banks giving Ovi pointers on how not to drown while Zara and Binita danced around each other behind him.

If you keep backing up, you might as well run away, Zara snapped, slashing at Binita with a stick. She had several inches on the shorter girl, and the stick went right over her head when she ducked.

If I get closer, you'll just stab me! Binita wailed.

That's the idea, Zara replied, lunging forward. Binita danced away, scrambling up the nearest tree awkwardly. *How are we supposed to practice if you're up there?* Binita only stuck out her tongue, and Zara growled in frustration.

Zara, you can swim, right? Kareem asked.

She spun around to glare at him. *Yes, why?*

Switch with me, he said, motioning to Ovi. He wasn't getting anywhere with him at the moment anyway. Ovi had an unfortunate habit of inhaling at the exact moment he should be holding his breath.

Kareem went over to the tree Binita lounged in like a cat, debating how to coax her down. If only he had a mouse or a lizard...

It had been two weeks since they agreed to practice together, and Kareem had to agree that they were at least trying. He glanced back at Zara, who was telling Ovi he looked like a wet rat. It wasn't a perfect situation, but they would get better. The first real skirmish was coming up in a little over a week. If they won, they would have the opportunity to go on an unsupervised assignment as a team.

It was one step closer to becoming venari.

If they lost, they would have to wait months until the next skirmish. Kareem still had a mind to finish venari training as quickly as possible. He just had to find a way to rally three other people to do it. He had been watching the other pupils during his classes, looking for weaknesses. The problem was that they didn't know the exact rules of the skirmish until the day of. So instead, Kareem decided to have them focus on skills they would need on assignment. Physical combat was always good, and getting Ovi to swim wouldn't be a bad idea. Zara and Binita had had a fairly tame assignment in Norway. The most important thing they learned was about other climates, which was something Kareem hadn't actually thought of. Despite all that, he thought they were doing pretty well.

Binita, if you practice two rounds with me, I'll give you my sister's feather collection. He glanced up at her in the tree.

She arched a brow. *What kind of feathers?*

He huffed. *I have no idea. Ones she collected from dead birds?*

Her feet thumped to the ground. *Deal.*

He spent the next half an hour trying to teach her how to hold her ground in a fight. Not that he was an expert, but he at least *tried* to win a fight instead of evading it altogether. It's not like she'd be able to sit in a tree to avoid an ubir.

Remembering the ubir brought Neelan to mind. Kareem hadn't seen him since he left on assignment over two weeks ago. He still wanted to talk to him about what happened in Jaipur, to apologize. That and he had questions about future assignments. There had to be a good way to organize his team when they went out, like some sort of plan.

We should start coming up with a strategy for the skirmishes, he said aloud instead, arcing his arm in slow motion so Binita had time to block. *I'm not sure what other teams are doing, but it would be nice to be prepared.*

I can do a little recon and try to find out, Binita said. *I know some of the people on the other teams. Then we can strategize with the intel.*

Okay, but can we do that tomorrow? Zara said from her spot on the bank. *I'm tired of watching Ovi drown.* True to her assessment, Ovi was sputtering behind her in two feet of water.

Yeah, we can do it tomorrow, Kareem said, trying not to laugh.

Jalla calls the shots, mostly, Aryan said. *The rest of us just do what she says. She's pretty good at it.*

I don't think that's going to apply to my team, Kareem exhaled. He was eating lunch with Aryan and Waqas the following day. Binita had promised to do some digging on the other teams, but Kareem wasn't incapable of asking questions.

All of us have very different personalities, he added.

That's the best part! Waqas exclaimed. *You see, listen here,* he said as Kareem slurped a spoonful of his soup. The vegetables were tender and lightly spiced. *My team had the same problems as yours. We were all so different, we were butting heads at the beginning, and everyone wanted to be in charge. What helped was figuring out what we were good at and sticking to that role. Yes, we all had opinions on what to do, but we each operated like a separate cog in a larger wheel. Everything worked smoothly after we figured that bit out.*

Waqas leaned back, looking satisfied with his elderly advice.

That's not a terrible idea, Kareem admitted.

Yeah, unless there is a possible coup within your team, Aryan added slyly.

Kareem, thinking he meant his team, looked up sharply. *What do you mean?*

Samira heard from Inaam that her team is not doing well at all. She thinks they are going to fail, Aryan said. *She's afraid to tell other people, though, so don't say anything.*

Why does she think that? Kareem asked.

Apparently, Aryan said, pointing his spoon, *Caden is the team leader, but everything he does is coming straight from Idris, and it's hurting them badly. He has the girls running drills all night and acting like servants.*

I've seen Idris. That kid's an eel, Waqas said sourly.

Aryan nodded. *Inaam thinks Faiza is a much better leader, but every time she stands up to Caden, he and Idris practically threaten her. It's a mess.*

Hmm, Kareem hummed in thought. *Can't she talk to their mentor?*

Aryan shrugged. *No idea. That's all I heard.*

Hey, have either of you seen my mentor Neelan? Kareem asked suddenly.

No, Waqas said. *I haven't. Why? I thought he was on assignment.*

Kareem leaned back in his chair. Why was the assignment taking so long? *No reason, I was just looking for him.*

KAREEM MADE it to his mental conditioning class and still hadn't gotten Neelan out of his mind. He had heard Savar say the assignment should be short. Had he returned and left again already? Even so, he should still have checked in on them. It had been nearly two and a half weeks. Where was he?

Kareem, your Aura should not be pulsating like a human disco ball. Laban's dark eyes stared him down from across the room. Kareem didn't know what a disco ball was, but he focused on his meditation again. All Anunnaki could reveal their Auras to each other any time they pleased, each having a unique color. Kareem's was a dark blue that fluctuated when he was deep in thought, apparently.

Laban liked to use Auras to know when pupils' minds started to wander during meditation. It was one of the few times Kareem saw so many Auras at once. Most people never revealed theirs except during times of prayer or celebration. It didn't take Kareem long to stabilize his own, thanks to Binita's teachings. Oddly enough, her eccentric list of mental exercises seemed to be helping. Laban continued on his walk around the room as soon as Kareem focused again.

Kareem glanced over to see Binita giving him a thumbs up.

The rest of the class passed at its usual mind-numbing pace. Binita started telling him about the information she had found, but Kareem promised to meet her and the others up on the roof in a minute. He needed to talk to Laban.

As the other pupils filed out of the room, Kareem made his way to the back.

Questions about how to improve your focus, Kareem? Laban asked as he came over.

Uh, no, sir, Kareem replied. *I was wondering if you've seen my mentor Neelan. I need to talk to him.*

Laban's head tilted just a fraction, hesitating. *Is it something important? If so, you can talk to any of your instructors or the other mentors.*

Kareem didn't want to talk about what happened in Jaipur with Laban, and he didn't want to sound paranoid, either. So instead, he just said, *Ah, no, I just wanted to know where he was.*

Laban frowned. *If you focus on yourself instead of the whereabouts of others, your mental focus might improve,* he said with a raise of his eyebrows.

Right, Kareem said, trying not to roll his eyes. *Good point.*

Kareem left the room, heading straight for the stairs. Laban's response had irked him. It was clear he knew something about Neelan, and if there was something to know and they hadn't told Kareem and his team, then it was probably bad. Tejas had said some of the Anunnaki citizens had gone missing lately. Was it possible that a venari had gone missing as well? After seeing the gentle, patient Neelan become a deadly venari the moment Ovi had been in trouble, Kareem doubted it would be easy for someone to have hurt him. He also didn't seem like the type to just disappear.

He went to the supply closet on the second floor, where he had discovered the ladder leading up to the door to the roof. Kareem climbed the rungs as quickly as he could, shoving the top door open until it clattered backward. Binita, Ovi, and Zara were all there already, sitting in a circle. Kareem marched up to them, interrupting their conversation.

Has anyone seen Neelan at all since we got back from our assignments?

They all stared at him for a moment and then at each other. *I haven't,* Binita said. Ovi shook his head as well.

I was actually wondering the same thing, Zara added, crossing her arms. *I have been meaning to talk to him, but he hasn't been in his room... or anywhere, apparently.*

Kareem furrowed his brows. *I've asked a few people, and none have seen him. But I just asked Laban as well, and the way he answered made it sound like he knew something.*

Knew something, Ovi repeated. *What is there to know?*

Exactly! Kareem exclaimed.

I'm not following, Binita said.

I've heard from several people that some of the Anunnaki have gone missing over the last few months. They are mainly part of the first wave of people living in human cities. But now Neelan hasn't come back, and it seemed like Laban was hiding something, Kareem explained.

I've heard the same thing, Ovi added grimly.

Well, something is definitely going on then, Zara said, getting to her feet. *If we've all noticed something, then it's true. Should we go to Savar then?*

There's no way he would tell us, Kareem said with a shake of his head.

Binita cleared her throat. *I mean... he does have those files on all the venari's whereabouts in his office on the left side of the second shelf.*

They all just stared at her, her big eyes blinking innocently.

Binita, Kareem said tentatively, *are you going to tell us how you know that?* His voice ended up an octave higher than he intended.

Nope.

He sighed, sitting down. *We better come up with a plan, then. If Savar catches us, we're as good as expelled.*

Ovi gaped. *We're actually going to break into his office?*

Binita grinned, and Zara sat back down eagerly.

Yes, Kareem said, looking around at them. *We need to find out what happened to Neelan. But first, Binita, do you think you can find those files again if we get you in?*

Binita's widening grin told him all he needed to know.

CHAPTER 14

IN THE NAME OF STEALTH

Kareem rolled his shoulder back, narrowly missing Binita's fist. His eyes were trained on the balcony above the training ring and less so on the girl trying—and failing—to land a single punch.

I almost had you, she said, getting back into her stance, left foot forward and right foot back.

We're not really here to spar, remember? Zara said from a few feet away. She was doing an excellent job making Ovi dodge unnecessarily in the sand to avoid her rapid-fire kicks.

I know, Binita said, *but might as well make it look good.* She threw her fist forward, overextending, and Kareem just ducked to the side. Despite the Aurastones that glowed around the ring constantly, the darkness of night was making the shadows grow up on the balcony. Kareem had to squint to see Savar's office from where he was.

The sun had set a while ago, and they were the only ones in the pit, the other pupils and venari mostly in their rooms. A pale blue light showed from under Savar's office door. He was still in there. They couldn't wait another day; Neelan had been gone too long, and they had to know what had happened.

Okay, Zara, Kareem said, *do it slowly now. Just a little at a time, so it's not too noticeable.*

She nodded, and her sparring with Ovi slowed until it barely looked like they were concentrating. A moment later, goosebumps broke out over Kareem's arms and up his spine as chilly air filled the space.

Tamp it down a bit, he said quietly. Zara sent a sharp glare at him, but the air was only mildly colder now. He hadn't brought it up to her that her stamina had gotten better ever since their fight by her house. On average, she could hold it for close to four minutes now. For that time, the four of them pretended to spar while keeping an eye on Savar's office.

The minutes crept by, but the office door didn't open.

Are you sure the cold makes him tired? Ovi asked Binita dubiously. He was moving his body in nothing more than a slow circle, barely pretending to spar.

Binita gave a firm nod. *He always goes back to his room on the nights that it's colder. Maybe his bones ache,* she said with a shrug.

The usual warmth of the city was starting to ease back in. *A little longer, Zara,* Kareem muttered. The door still hadn't opened. The plan was a long shot at best, resting mostly on Binita's secretly acquired knowledge—which she refused to share its origin—and luck. It was apparent this was not the first time she had snuck into Savar's office. Kareem made a mental note to have a very serious chat with her in the future.

I'm trying, Zara hissed back at him. The cold increased but only a little. Savar's office was just off the training ring on the second floor, so Zara's cold should range close enough to dip the temperature inside. If it didn't work, he'd have to come up with a far craftier plan than this one.

The door cracked open, letting pale blue light out that quickly went dark. The four of them all glanced up to see Savar exiting his office, shutting and locking the door behind him. They went back to sparring, but he didn't pay attention to them in the pit. It wasn't against the rules to be out late at night, but few students had the energy to practice more after a day with Hessa's training.

Kareem looked to the others, nodding once. As agreed, Zara headed for the stairs to tail Savar at a distance, bringing some of the cold with her, hopefully keeping him tired and ready for sleep. Ovi followed Zara after a moment to be backup if needed. Kareem and Binita continued their fake sparring for a few more minutes in case any late-nighters cared to stroll by the ring. Sure enough, a middle-aged venari passed through the halls that rang by the sand, giving them a look filled with pity.

Midnight training, huh? he said, eyes their form. *You kids are going to need it.* Kareem and Binita just gave awkward grimaces, and the venari moved on. Another minute went by, and when no one else was around, they dropped their facade and made their way up to the office.

Binita hadn't been clear about how she was going to be able to get Kareem into the office, but the last thing he had expected was for her to pull a makeshift key out of the folds of her gray uniform. It looked made of the same limestone the rest of the city was built out of and roughly cut, as if by hand. Kareem's eyebrows rose to his hairline, but he just shook his head.

They would be having a *very* serious talk in the future. What other secrets did this girl have? She had least had the audacity to look guilty for a split second before the usual carefree demeanor took over, and she unlocked the office as if it were her own, pushing the door open to let Kareem inside.

I'll wait out here, she said. *If I knock, it means someone is coming. They're on that shelf there,* she said, pointing to one of the mid-level shelves on one of the bookcases.

Kareem nodded. *I'll be quick.* He slipped inside and shut the door quietly. It was odd seeing the sparse room without Savar in it. Kareem's heartbeat actually started to pick up, realizing what he was doing was definitely something he would get expelled for. There would be nowhere to hide if Savar decided to come back, even if Binita warned him in time. He would just need to be quick about it.

The light of a small Aurastone lit the room in a faint glow. Kareem found several stacks of large cloth-bound books stacked on the shelf Binita had indicated. There were at least twenty of them, and each was nearly three inches thick. Hoping there was some kind of system, Kareem slid one off the top of a stack and flopped the pages open. Inside was a ledger filled with dates, names, locations, and additional notes. Binita had been correct. After looking over the first page, it was clearly a record of all assignments.

The knowledge of where the ubir were had always come from seers. The old Grand Elder Hakim had provided most of the information for nearly two hundred years before he died, and now the queen's adviser Eta and her team of young seers did the same. The information they gave was always minimal. A city, maybe a first name, and rarely other details. Each vision on an ubir was recorded here, and the subsequent venari that was sent out, when they were sent, when they returned, and the status of the ubir. The dates on this book went further back, as if the book was written starting from the back and working forward. The front page ended on a date two years ago.

On a hunch, Kareem set that book down and went to the far left pile, taking the book off the top. He was correct, the first third of the book was empty, and the first page with writing had dates from just yesterday and the two venari that were sent out. He flipped back a few pages to the day Neelan was sent out and leaned toward the Auralight lamp to see better. A cold feeling settled in his stomach after finding the record.

Toronto, Canada / Adonal – 3 missing AN / Neelan Qureshi sent: 10/6/26 returned:

Kareem glanced over the other records. All had notes of return dates or check-ins. Neelan had neither. And what did that note mean? 'Adonal – 3 missing AN.' Adonal must have been the name of the ubir, but what about 'AN'? That had to mean missing people. None of the other records had a similar note. All other records since then had return dates, but it was now the 25th of October, and Neelan still wasn't back. Had something happened to him? Why was there no other note? The empty return date sat there on the page like a forgotten doodle from weeks past. Why hadn't Savar *done* something?

Kareem's head was spinning as he stared at the page. Maybe if he dug through the stacks of books, he would find something about the missing people. It was possible the ubir were behind it, but then why did none of the other venari find anything when the ubir were captured? Flipping through more pages, all the other venari were accounted for. Only Neelan hadn't returned. And why had Neelan been sent alone? Were they not supposed to go in pairs?

Shoving the book back in its spot, Kareem started to dig through the pile. As he reached the bottom, he heard the door hand twist. His heart went straight into his throat.

This was it. He was going to be discovered! There was nowhere to hide, so Kareem stood like a caught burglar in the center of the room as the door was pushed open. An unfamiliar boy with a familiar set of curls poked his head in. Who was this?

What's taking you so long? the boy said.

Kareem froze, confused. *Um, what?*

I told you to be quick! Someone is going to see me.

Kareem understood as Binita's features melted back into her

own, and he exhaled long and loud. His poor heart was trying to escape from his chest. *I'm done,* he said. *Let's go.*

The halls were dark as he and Binita started toward his room. The four of them had agreed to meet back thereafter. Binita kept glancing at him out of the corner of her eye.

Well? What did you find?

I'll tell you when we're all in the room.

They turned a corner down to Kareem's hallway and nearly ran face-first into Hessa. She looked down with raised brows as the two of them opened their mouths like fish. *Shouldn't you two be in bed?* she asked. *You are aware we have training in the morning, correct?* The Auralight in the hall cast her suspicious features in an eerie blue glow.

Yes, ma'am, Kareem blurted out, his words steadier than expected. *We were actually just doing some late-night training in the ring.*

Mhm, Hessa said. *I expected you to be back there before sunrise. To bed with you.* She jerked her chin down the hall.

Kareem and Binita mumbled their agreements and hurried to his room, shutting the door behind them. Zara and Ovi weren't back yet, though. They sat in silence, waiting for them to return, and just as Kareem was starting to worry, Ovi pushed the door open with Zara right behind him.

What took you so long? Kareem said, getting to his feet.

Before Zara could retort, Ovi said, *We didn't know how long you needed.*

Well, did Savar notice you? Kareem asked.

Zara tossed her hair over her shoulder and sat next to Binita on one of the beds. *Of course not. What did you find out? I assume you didn't get caught.*

We ran into Hessa on our way back, but I don't think she suspected too much, Binita said, going over to Ovi's bookshelf and thumbing through the volumes. *So where is Neelan?* She glanced over her shoulder at him.

Kareem frowned, thinking about the ledger. *Just as we thought. Neelan left over two and a half weeks ago and hasn't returned. All the other venari are either accounted for or have returned and left on new assignments. He definitely should have been back by now.*

That's it? Zara said. *We already knew that.*

The note in the ledger was odd, though, Kareem said. *It said he was in Vancouver, and then a name—Adonal—who I assume is the ubir. But then it said, '3 missing AN'.*

It's the missing people, Ovi said immediately. They all turned to look at him. *'AN' is the abbreviation the scholars use for Anunnaki. And if he didn't specify venari or humans, then it is referring to the first wavers that went out to live in the human cities.*

So... what? Binita said. *The ubir kidnapped them?*

Out of revenge against the Anunnaki? Zara questioned. *How would they even know about the other Anunnaki? It's not like there are that many of them.*

I've thought about it, and I think not everything was written down, Kareem said, crossing his arms. *Those ledgers were meticulous. There is no way he just forgot about Neelan or forgot to write in additional notes. Also, Neelan was sent alone, which never happens anymore.*

He knows something, then, Binita confirmed.

I think so. Kareem stared at the ground.

We need to ask him directly then, Zara said, mirroring Kareem's position. *We should talk to Savar and ask him outright where Neelan is. Make him admit Neelan is missing. It sounds like they aren't doing anything about this. Does the queen know what's going on? This sounds like neglect to me.*

Kareem expected the others to argue with her, but they kept silent. They were all in agreement then, so Kareem just nodded.

I'll talk to him tomorrow.

. . .

IF YOU THROW both your arms up, you're leaving your middle exposed, Hessa said, pulling one of Kareem's arms closer to his chest, forcing him to tuck the spear in his armpit.

They were back in the training ring, all traces of Zara's chilly air long gone. Sweat soaked through gray uniforms as they ran drills with obsidian-tipped spears. It was rare they got to use real ones instead of practice poles. Hessa had them spaced far apart as she, Amol, and Laban paced around, correcting forms as they went.

Kareem kept his one arm tucked closer and spun on his heel before shuffling sideways in the sand. He glanced up at the sun that was almost to its midday position above the ring. He had decided to confront Savar over their break and find out what was really going on. They deserved to know where their mentor was. Kareem kept imagining what sort of horrid ubir would be able to take Neelan down. The image of his enraged face in Jaipur as he defended Ovi had Kareem thinking up the worst sort of ubir. And if it wasn't the ubir...where was he then?

To his left, Samira paused her forms to look at Kareem. *Your form actually looks great today, Kareem. Have you guys been practicing?*

Spaced out around the ring, Ovi, Zara, and Binita *were* looking better than usual. They weren't the most naturally gifted, but they all had determined looks on their faces as they ran through the drills.

He caught Faiza nodding in appreciative agreement as he said, *A little.*

Actually getting afraid you might not graduate? Caden said with a chuckle. He moved to the other side of Samira. His spear swung in starts and stops, nearly imperceptible zaps of electricity popping near his fingers. *About time you realized you weren't cut out for this.*

Across from him, Idris had a faint smile for once. Out of all of this year's pupils, Idris had the most natural ability with weapons. His movements were swift and precise, almost cold. Kareem could see him imagining plunging the spear through his enemy with hardly a blink.

Samira started to retort, but Kareem didn't hear any of them as Hessa called for them to stop and put their spears away. They were done for the day. He glanced across the sand, making eye contact with his team. They all nodded in encouragement, so he placed his spear on the rack and made his way for the stairs as the rest of them dallied.

Kareem almost felt guilty when he knocked on Savar's door, knowing his team had a literal key to the office. That was replaced by a low hum of anger. They had no right to keep them in the dark about Neelan. And it didn't seem like they were doing anything about it. Zara was right. Did the queen know that a venari had gone missing now?

Come in, a voice called.

Kareem stepped in and found a venari woman with a deep scar on her neck talking with Savar. *Go in pairs,* he said, handing her a sheet of papers. The woman nodded and glanced down at Kareem on her way out.

The stacks of ledgers sat right behind Savar, but Kareem had his eyes locked on the man as he scribbled notes in another, smaller booklet. *What can I do for you, Kareem?* he said, finally glancing up. He didn't seem to know someone had broken into his office the night before.

I want to know where Neelan is, Kareem said firmly, crossing his arms over his chest. He wouldn't allow himself to feel any more guilt. He was right to be worried about his mentor.

Savar blinked at him and sat back. *He's on assignment. Did you need to talk with someone about your training? There are many other—*

I apologize for interrupting, but I'm not here about myself; I'm here about Neelan. He should have been back by now. We haven't seen him in weeks, and everything we've been taught says an assignment shouldn't last that long. If he didn't have the permanent venari extension on his tattoo, he could very well be human by now for being gone so long.

Savar just looked at him for far longer than was comfortable, the jowls of his cheeks drooping to form a constant frown. His eyes softened suddenly. *I can see you are afraid for your mentor, but those fears are unfounded. Yes, you are correct. Under normal circumstances, this would be too long for Neelan to be gone. But Neelan has been a venari for many years now and occasionally is sent on far more advanced assignments than young pupils.* His voice dropped an octave as he finished, the words landing like stones.

Kareem wouldn't be swayed easily, though. *Shouldn't we be worried at all? I've heard from several people that some of the Anunnaki have gone missing out in the human cities. What if Neelan has gone missing too? Shouldn't we—*

Savar cut him off with a wave of his hand. *I'd advise you not to listen to loose gossip. If there was something to worry about, I or the queen herself would have made a public announcement. Neelan is accounted for, so your concern is misplaced. Young pupils have no place digging into the matters of adults.*

Kareem closed his mouth. It was a clear finality of the conversation.

Now, Savar said, *go back to your lessons, and Neelan will come to you when he returns.*

Knowing he had been fully dismissed, Kareem left the office, closing the door and already trying to decide what to do next. He had a sinking feeling something terrible was happening.

CHAPTER 15

STRENGTH IN UNITY

Kareem sat with his back against a low wall that ran around the edge of the roof. Zara paced back and forth between him and Ovi and Binita, who sat across from him. He had just finished telling them what Savar had said earlier that day, which was practically nothing and somehow everything.

We're going to do something, right? Zara asked.

Kareem looked up to find she had stopped pacing and was staring at him along with Ovi and Binita. It was a momentary shock, but he realized how different everything was compared to the first day of training. They were all looking to him for answers.

Which meant he needed to have them.

Yes, I'm just trying to think of what the best course of action would be, he said slowly.

Should we go to the queen? Ovi said. *It sounds like Savar and the other instructors are hiding something. Maybe the queen doesn't know what is going on.*

Zara shook her head, resuming her pacing. *She won't listen to us.*

That's assuming you can get an audience, Binita added.

I think we should go ourselves, Kareem finally said after a silence had lapsed too long. Again, they all stopped to stare at him.

You mean go to Canada? Zara said, her face twisting in incredility.

Yes, Kareem said, getting to his feet and walking in a slow circle. *I mean, between the four of us, we can at least track down the ubir, even if we don't catch it. But we can also scout the area and see if we find him or any clues. If the ubir doesn't have Neelan and we can't find anything, then we come back. Simple as that.*

Zara, who had relinquished her pacing duty to Kareem, now leaned against the wall, the sun a setting halo behind her. *I'm in,* she said firmly.

Kareem was expecting to have to convince her, but that was surprisingly easy.

Yeah, it can't hurt to take a trip there, Binita said. *As long as we don't try to actually bring the ubir in, I think we should be fine.*

Ovi made a faint choking noise, his face a mask of pain. *Ovi, you definingly do not need to come considering what you went through last time,* Kareem offered. He wouldn't dare let Ovi get hurt again because of him.

I'm more worried about how we'll even manage that, Ovi said, shoulders hunching over his skinny body as he rested elbows on his knees.

We have to win the skirmish, Kareem said, still thinking it through.

Zara scoffed, sliding down the wall to sit on the roof. *Okay, never mind. He's an idiot, and this plan is dumb.*

Kareem rolled his eyes at her. *I already talked to my friend Waqas who is a venari. He said the winners of the skirmishes always get two days off training afterward. We can use that time to leave without anyone noticing we're gone.*

And what about the ink? Ovi asked. *Mine's already worn off, and only venari get the permanent stuff. We can't leave the city without it.*

Kareem glanced at Binita. *We steal it,* she said with a grin.

Zara exhaled forcefully. *So if we happen to win the skirmish and just happen to steal a bottle of ink, what do we do? Just wander down the mountain, knock on the Ummanu's door, and say, 'Four for Canada, please?'*

Yep, Kareem said. It was actually starting to sound like a solid plan to him.

I still think someone is going to find out, Ovi added.

We can't abandon Neelan, Kareem said firmly. *It's dangerous, but we have to do it. I'm not forcing anyone to come. Just agree to help win the skirmish.*

It's in a week, Zara said. *How are we going to win? Cheat?*

No, Kareem insisted, facing them. *We just have to be better. I heard one of the other teams isn't doing well. If there is one, then there are more. We can find out as much as possible to use against them in the skirmish and train ourselves in the meantime.*

This is insane, Zara said. *The chances of us winning are close to zero.* She sighed in the most dramatic way possible. *Okay,* she said, *let's give it a shot.*

The others nodded in agreement with varying degrees of enthusiasm. *Let's agree to just focus as much as possible this next week and meet at the stream tomorrow after lessons. Deal?*

Binita and Ovi agreed, but Zara interjected. *If we are going to put ourselves in mortal danger, I need to do something tomorrow after lessons. I'll meet you there the next day.*

Kareem caught her eye, which was as frigid as normal, daring him to object. He didn't, instead just giving her an approving nod. He would let her tell the others about her mother on her own time —if she ever did.

Kareem and his team spent the next several days wearing themselves down to the bone both during lessons and outside of them. They put as much effort as possible during Hessa's body-numbing drills and focused hard on the afternoon lessons. In between, they decided to divide and conquer, talking with their friends on other teams to weasel any information out of them that may help. They made it a point to meet briefly in the halls between lessons to trade information or add to their plan.

In the middle of the week, Kareem was tucked into a side hallway with Zara and Ovi. They had circled back to the ink and how they were going to obtain it. Both Ovi and Zara thought it too risky to attempt breaking into Savar's office for a second time.

We don't have that kind of luck, Zara said. Not for the first time, Kareem wondered how much easier his life would be if he had Tejas's abilities.

We have to, he said. *We can't go without the ink. We'd last maybe a day beyond the barrier before we lost our abilities and memories. There's no way we'd make it back in time.* Kareem cursed himself for not grabbing a bottle while he had been in Savar's office. It would have been right there on the shelf.

The hallway next to them suddenly filled with a stream of pupils walking by between their lessons. Binita ejected herself from the crowd and came up to them. *Anything new?*

We're trying to decide how to get the ink, Kareem said, leaning against the wall. *They don't want to break in again.*

Actually, that's what I came to talk to you about, Binita said, grinning. *I found out that Savar isn't the only one who has it.*

Well, who else would? Zara asked. *Another venari?*

Binita shook her head. *The permanent ink was made by a group of scholars. They keep a vial of it in the library, so I'm assuming they have the temporary stuff there as well. We can't use the permanent, or someone will definitely find out we left.*

In the library? Ovi asked. *Where?*

In one of the offices upstairs, Binita said. She scrunched up her face. *I'm pretty sure I know where it is. I've seen them there before. They do all sorts of research for the queen.*

Kareem nodded, getting excited. *It would be much easier to break into the library. People are in there late all the time. We just have to do it at night.*

Ovi nodded. *That's... actually a good idea. I say we do it tonight.* Kareem didn't miss the way he looked at Binita with confused admiration.

Perfect, Kareem said. *We'll meet at the river after lessons and head there after the sun sets.*

THE FOUR OF them hurried through the city gate, noting the warriors that stood watch up above. Being outside the city at night wasn't against the law, but they were all on edge. Few people were out this late, and Kareem was more worried about sneaking back into the house of the venari instead of breaking into a library office.

The library was an imposing building of limestone that sat on the easter edge of the central plaza, only a few streets away from the house of the venari. Kareem had been there many times gathering books when he was younger but always found the dusty books and scrolls to be a bit eerie. It might have had something to do with how quiet it was in there. It was always open since many scholars worked needlessly through the night to fuel whatever obsession they were focused on at the moment, but it was much quieter when they stepped through the front doors so late in the evening.

The building had been almost entirely rebuilt after the Battle of Rhapta nearly destroyed it five years ago. The main floor had vaulted ceilings that hung over a range of low tables. Further back, a forest of shelves began on the second floor and looked over the first with another set of shelves.

One or two scholars were sitting at the front tables and didn't look up as the four of them quietly hurried to the back and into the maze of shelves. Toward the back of the building, a wide staircase spiraled up to the second floor. As they went up, Binita said, *I heard there are subterranean archives somewhere under the building. Wouldn't it be cool if we found them?*

Ovi shook his head. *They sealed those up years ago. A rebel group was found hiding down there.*

I don't think that's—

Shh! Zara interjected. *So where is this room, Binita?*

The second floor looked out over a balcony on the right, and the left went further back into a maze of more shelves interspersed with doors between the stacks. *I think this way,* she said, leading them back.

There was only one other scholar up here, nose deep into a pile of scrolls. They passed shelf after shelf as Binita glanced at the doors. Even further back and to the left, a seemingly anonymous door stood closed between the ancient history section.

I think this is it, she said.

Okay, Kareem said, glancing back at Zara and Ovi. *You two keep watch. Pretend you're looking at—*

Yes, yes, Zara said. *We're professionals at looking inconspicuous. Just hurry up.* They disappeared around the corner.

Kareem turned back to see Binita already had the door open. Wasn't it even locked? Did the scholars really not expect anyone to just walk in? He followed her inside and found a long room filled with tables. There were two more rooms at opposite ends that connected to this one; all were dark except for faint Aurastone lamps. They were a disaster at best. Papers, scrolls, and books were scattered all over, with many of the papers stuck to the walls. Boxes of writing utensils, paints, and brushes sat haphazardly with crumpled balls of paper, bowls, and piles of dead plants.

Does a chimpanzee work here? Kareem muttered to himself.

Binita had already picked through to the opposite end of the room and was digging in an upright chest filled with small drawers. She was pulling them out and slamming them shut just as fast. *Here!* she whispered suddenly, holding up a handful of vials.

Kareem hurried over to her. The small vials of dark liquid were even labeled with a date of creation and permanent versus temporary. The scholars *really* needed to consider adding some measure of security to this room.

Binita pocketed one of the temporary ink bottles into her uniform, along with the needles required to do the tattooing before closing the chest. Hopefully, the scatterbrained scholar that worked here wouldn't notice.

Kareem glanced at Binita as she closed the chest with an exasperated sigh. *Binita, we really need to talk about how you knew this was here. First, Savar's office, now this?*

She glanced sharply at him in a way that Zara usually did, but the expression was gone before he could understand it. *The others are waiting. Let's go.* She was already hurrying across the room and out the door.

They found Zara leaning against a shelf, barely hiding her boredom as Ovi stood next to her, a volume wide open and his eyes scanning the page. At least he didn't need to try too hard to look inconspicuous.

Did you get it? Zara asked when she saw them.

Yep, Binita said, her normal, mischievous self back. Kareem would work on that later. Right now, they needed to get back to the house of the venari.

They slipped back through the silent stacks of books, down the stairs, and back out the front door. Only one of the scholars remained as they passed. Outside, the crescent moon hung above them as they scurried through the streets. Kareem led them to the back door of the building, which was rarely busy. His heart thrummed in his chest, but there was no one waiting for them inside. It was practically a miracle that they walked through the halls without seeing a soul.

The boys and girls went their separate ways, and soon Kareem found himself safely back in his bed. He stayed up a while longer, reflecting on all the ways his team had been changing into something new over the past few weeks. But would it be enough to win the skirmish? They had to; otherwise, Neelan would be on his own.

CHAPTER 16

THE SKIRMISH

Kareem and Ovi stepped down into the training ring just before dawn, finding Zara and Binita already there. Other pupils were there, as well as venari that casually hung around the upper banisters. A sense of nervousness and excitement thrummed through the area. Today was the first real skirmish, and Kareem refused to lose. Somehow, he was both in the same position and an entirely different one from two months ago.

Hessa stood in the middle of the ring; her hood pulled up like usual. Amol and Laban stood near her, waiting for the pupils to arrive. Around the ring, five colored flags were tied at intervals around the banister posts with equally colored stones about the size of a melon sitting in the sand below them.

The morning sunlight was barely starting to creep into the building when all the pupils arrived, and Hessa stepped forward. *Good morning, pupils. You all know what today is; your first official skirmish.*

If anyone was still talking, they quieted to listen to her.

Today we will get to see what two months of training has done to improve your performance both individually and as a team. The objective will be different this time. She gestured around the ring. *There are flags posted around the ring for each of your teams with a similar colored stone. The objective today is to acquire the stones of the other four teams while defending yours. The first team to collect all five stones will be the winner. Simple, yes?*

Pained looks crossed the faces of the pupils, and a few of the venari up above chuckled. Hessa kicked a pile of wooden poles at her feet. *We won't be using obsidian weapons today, but each of you will be allowed a single stave. You are welcome to use your abilities—within reason. I would advise you not to kill each other. That would be counterproductive to your training,* she said, mumbling the last part.

As you all know, she continued, *the winner of today's skirmish will be allowed to go on their first unsupervised assignment in a few weeks to hunt down an ubir as a team. This will be counted toward your graduation. As a more immediate reward, you will get a few days off to do as you choose, starting today. For the losers, you will have to try harder next time. Let's not waste time. Everyone, grab a stave and pick a flag.*

Kareem and his team grabbed a stave for each of them and found themselves standing under a blue flag with a blue stone at their feet. They didn't need to speak much as they had been planning for every possible scenario all week. Zara and Ovi would take a defensive position, guarding their stone, while Kareem and Binita would start on the offensive. Ovi wasn't ready to use his ability, and Kareem wouldn't push him. The other four teams grouped together under red, green, yellow, and purple flags. Pupils were bouncing on their toes and testing staves. There would be no hesitation like last time. Hessa and the other venari stepped out of the ring while other older pupils gathered with the venari. Kareem saw Zaid and Savar arrive up above as well.

In true Hessa fashion, she shouted *Begin!* without warning.

Chaos erupted, and sand flew as pupils dashed across the ring in every direction. Binita ran to the yellow stone, which was guarded by a team with few offensive abilities. Kareem went straight across to the purple stone that was currently guarded by Aryan and his team leader Jalla. He had found out Jalla's ability was a long set of steel claws that extended from her fingernails nearly six inches. She had her stave gripped in her hands as well and crouched as Kareem sprinted toward her. As expected, Aryan was using his ability to form a moat of mud around the purple stone.

Jalla whipped her stave at him as he came close, but Kareem caught it, reaching out to touch her wrist at the same time, sticking her hands to the stave. Jalla tried to shift her hands but found she couldn't, so Kareem yanked her to the side, and she toppled into the sand. He turned to find Aryan distracted by Tarun, so he took a running leap over the half-formed moat and snatched the purple stone up. It was heavier than he expected, but he had months of Hessa's relentless training to aid him.

In just a few moments, he was back to his own team's flag. Zara was defending against two girls, expertly twirling her stave, whacking them sharply. Ovi looked grim as he held his own stave behind her, so Kareem tossed the purple stone to him, and he dropped it next to the blue one.

Kareem! Zara shouted. *Help Binita!*

It was hard to focus amid the shouts and cheers in the building, and Kareem whirled around. He scanned the writhing mass of pupils and found Binita backing frantically away from an advancing Faiza. She had lost her stave already, but Kareem saw why.

In her arms was the red stone.

Behind her, Samira and another boy were closing in as well. Kareem hurried forward and shouted, *Binita! Throw it!*

Her curly head spun to find him several yards away, and she hurtled it roughly in his direction. Kareem had to run forward to get in line with the arc of the stone. As it was coming down, the view of the stone distorted and changed, like looking through frosted glass.

Was something wrong with his eyes?

He panicked, and the stone fell into his chest with a sick thud, sending him to the ground. Pain spread like wildfire across his chest as he rubbed his eyes. He couldn't see the stone clearly, just a red ball of a harshly distorted mirage.

Hands came and grabbed the red mirage, and Kareem looked up to find a sheepish Veer above him. *Sorry, Kareem,* he said before dashing away.

Binita reached Kareem's side and hauled him to his feet with her skinny arms. *Are you okay?* she asked.

Yeah, he said, already eyeing the ring to assess where the stones were. Inaam stood nearby, guarding the green and yellow stones. In the form of a huge panther, Mira guarded the red stone that Veer had somehow already lost while Idris advanced on her. Caden and Faiza were going after Kareem's stone on the other side of the ring. *Get ready. We're going to need a distraction soon. Like we practiced, okay?*

Binita nodded quickly.

Kareem started toward Inaam, and she moved to drop her hand to the ground. From experience, Kareem knew a shockwave would follow, but Caden's voice called Inaam from the side to stop. The girl hesitated but didn't see her teammate anywhere. Caden's voice kept shouting at her to stop and back up. Kareem, knowing Binita would hold the distraction as long as she could, used Inaam's confusion to hurry forward, knocking the girl back to the railing behind her and sticking her firmly to it. He scooped up the two stones and sprinted back toward his team.

Ovi was there alone now, and with only the purple stone to defend. Where was Zara?

Suddenly, the real Caden was before him, stave gone, but hands held out, crackling with electricity. Hessa said not to kill each other, but Kareem was certain Caden couldn't care less. He couldn't do anything either with the two stones in his arms.

This was going to be bad.

Kareem started to backpaddle when another stave cracked down between them squarely onto Caden's hands. Bone popped, and Caden screamed as Zara shouted at Kareem to hurry. Anunnaki healing would already be working to mend any fractures and bruises, but his hands would hurt for a while. He didn't stay to see the rage in the other boy's eyes, and Zara followed right behind him as he deposited the yellow and green stone next to the purple one.

Looking around, they had three of the five stones now. Both the blue and the red remained at opposite ends of the ring. With every additional stone they had, they would become more of a target. They would need to get the other two stones as fast as possible.

Most of the pupils were gathered around the blue stone that was held by the team Binita had gone after originally. They were the weakest of the five teams, and everyone assumed they would be the easiest to attack. But on the other end of the ring, Idris, Faiza, and Veer headed toward Mira, still in jaguar form. Veer was attempting to take Faiza down first, leaving Idris and Mira temporarily alone. Something about the way Idris was stalking closer to the cat left a sick feeling in Kareem's stomach. It was only amplified when Mira shook her head and yowled.

Idris was trying to control her.

Binita was running toward their group, and Kareem ran to meet her, grabbing her arm and dragging them toward Idris and Mira. Kareem didn't even have to point before Binita caught on and shouted in Caden's voice again to Idris, telling him to stop. Idris paused a moment, releasing Mira. At the same moment, Faiza had knocked Veer to the ground and was scrambling for the red stone.

Mira lunged for Idris, teeth bared. Kareem screamed at Binita to get the stone.

In the next moment, he slammed into Faiza with his entire body weight. It was like colliding with a brick wall. The breath whooshed out of Kareem's chest, but he and Faiza went down. She hardly seemed fazed and shoved him off, kicking her feet. Veer had gathered himself and came over to them as well, but Kareem twisted in the sand, grabbing for both Faiza's foot and Veer's, sticking them together. Veer yelped and went down again, attached to Faiza.

Kareem heard a vicious snarl, cutting fear into his heart, and turned to find Idris scrambling away from Mira after Binita, who was already halfway across the ring, dashing back and forth like a gecko. Idris wouldn't catch her. She was too far.

One stone left.

The other teams seemed to realize this and were streaming toward Ovi, Zara, and Binita. They would be overwhelmed within minutes, if not seconds. More and more pupils ran over to them until Kareem could no longer see his team, only the blue flag that hung above them.

He would need to move fast, or they wouldn't make it. Samira had the last stone now, ironically Kareem's own blue stone. She was leaping higher than should be possible around the ring like some graceful rabbit. Attempting to come up with a plan, Kareem left Faiza and Veer in the sand and ran after Samira. Other pupils were following her as well, and Kareem moved to cut her off her path.

Suddenly the room was enveloped in a baking heat followed by an incomparable weight on Kareem's body. He felt like every cell in his body was being forced *down,* and his heart strained under the weight. Both pupils and venari alike screamed as they were forced to the ground by the heat and pressure.

It was over as quickly as it had started.

What was *that?* Kareem dug his fingers into the sand, pulled himself upright, and craned his neck. The only person still standing was Zara, who braced herself in front of their four stones with her stave gripped in two hands. Kareem made a mental note to be terrified later because pupils were already starting to get up again. Just two yards from him, Samira had dropped the stone, and it sat in a patch of sunlit sand.

Kareem had it in his arms within seconds, sprinting toward his team. His lungs burned now, and all pupils had their eyes on him and descended on him in a wave. Kareem had a moment of déjà vu; he had been in this exact position the first day of training. He needed to do things differently this time.

Binita picked up a stave and started running toward him, swinging madly at the other pupils. She was missing more than she was hitting, but she proved an excellent distraction. It wasn't enough, though, and soon Kareem could only see the sea of pupils coming to get the stone. He dodged back and forth through the sand, trying to find a way through to his team. He was tired and running on panic now.

Suddenly Savar's voice boomed throughout the ring. *STOP!*

Everyone froze, and Kareem mentally thanked Binita, promising to give her all the feathers and mouse skulls he could find. While the pupils turned to look at Savar, who stood confused on the upper floor, Kareem ran. Pupils looked at him, unsure if the skirmish was still going or not. His team was within view, and apparently, he wasn't the only one who didn't stop.

He watched as Caden shoved Zara aside, grabbed the green stone, and turned. Kareem put total faith in his own team and hurtled the blue stone to Ovi just as the other pupils realized what had happened. At the same moment, Kareem turned sharply to cut Caden off. He couldn't let him get away and dove straight at him, barely grabbing him by the ankle. Caden went down hard and tried to yank his leg away, but Kareem's hand was stuck to his ankle, and Kareem hauled him back through the sand.

Heart beating wildly in his chest, Kareem didn't hesitate to rip the green stone from Caden and turned to throw it blindly toward Zara and Ovi.

Right as he released the stone, his body went ridged, his face and hands went numb, and his vision went black.

Kareem's heart stuttered in his chest. He couldn't feel anything for a second, and then it all rushed him at once. Pain coursed through his body from his hand that was still connected to Caden's ankle.

His vision came back, too bright. The other boy had reached down and grabbed Kareem by the wrist. Kareem saw the sparks of electricity as his lungs shuttered in his chest, and his breath came in gasps.

There were shouts of rage mixed with jubilant cheers. Kareem couldn't make sense of it for a moment, everything sounding far away. He saw someone rip Caden away at the same time Zara and Binita reached him, hauling him to his feet as his hearing came back, accompanied by a loud ringing. The electricity had stopped, but Kareem felt fried to a crisp.

He heard Hessa's voice coming from somewhere and blearily turned his head to see her shoving her way through the pupils. There was a mix of expressions on people's faces, from shock to anger to victory to concern. Hessa was none of these as she grabbed him by the shoulder.

Kareem, she said. *Are you all right?*

He nodded weakly.

Good, she said with a wide smile. *Because your team won.* More cheers erupted up on the banisters, and venari pounded on the rails.

Kareem gave her a lopsided grin back. They had won! He turned to catch the eyes of his teammates, who looked victorious but determined. While everyone else thought it was a simple skirmish, his team knew what this win meant.

They would be leaving tonight.

CHAPTER 17
INTO THE WORLD

Kareem had forgotten about the mosquitos. They bit at his face and arms and neck with the viscous enthusiasm of starved dogs. The four of them were quiet as they trudged down the mountain. The only sounds were of crunching leaves and the frequent slap as another mosquito died.

It had taken everything in Kareem to muster enough energy to complete nearly a million tasks that afternoon and evening after the skirmish. His ears still rang slightly from the electricity Caden had zapped him with, and his muscles ached from the skirmish. Hessa had told them they all had the afternoon's lessons off, and Kareem and his team were free to do as they chose for the next two days. Their actual assignment wouldn't be for several weeks.

They had wasted no time packing, planting alibis, and taking turns adding the temporary ink to their Anunnaki tattoos. The center of Kareem's back still tingled from where Ovi had stabbed him repeatedly with a needle. He prayed that they had grabbed the right ink; otherwise, they would be as good as human—and just as oblivious of the Anunnaki—within a day.

They had an unspoken agreement that they had to move

quickly. They needed to account for travel time, and they only had two days to be gone without anyone noticing. It was difficult, though, because they took a different path down the mountain to avoid any possible venari that were coming and going. They waited until well after the sun had set before they snuck out of the city. How the guard didn't see them, Kareem would never know.

The trip down passed quickly. They had managed to acquire one flashlight earlier in the week from a vendor at the market that sold human goods. It was barely enough to see by, but eventually, the trees thinned, and they found themselves standing in an empty parking lot on the side of a two-lane road.

Where do you think we are? Binita asked, looking around. There weren't any signs, and there were just shrubs and more trees on this side of the mountain.

Probably further west than we need to be, Ovi said. *I doubt we'll find a bus anytime soon.*

Yeah, Kareem said, seeing the empty road under the moon. *Let's just start walking.*

They walked single file down the road, hopefully toward Moshi and the portal. They had only brought a single bag each, just like the last time they left, plus the human clothes they had and the IDs they had received. Binita had even managed to snag a credit card from a venari's room; they would hardly notice. All the money they had was fake. The card would swipe, and transactions would be approved, but the vendors would never see the money in their accounts. Kareem had to be impressed at whichever Anunnaki had created them.

There was an odd sense of freedom that Kareem felt as he walked down the mountain this time. He had expected to feel guilty, but instead, he felt like he was standing on the edge of a cliff, a wild sensation that could easily result in death. He focused instead on what they needed to do to get to Toronto.

After about twenty minutes of walking, lights shone behind

them. A van with all the windows down was bumping along the road and slowed when it saw them. It was painted brightly and looked like an out-of-service shuttle. Inside was a man with his head shaved and a bright green t-shirt that looked out of the passenger side window.

He spoke in the local language, "Do you need a ride? I'm headed into town." He pointed vaguely up ahead.

Kareem was about to answer, but Zara cut in. "That would be excellent! Are you headed to Moshi?" They continued to converse back and forth, and Kareem realized she was much better at languages than he was. They found themselves sliding the door to the van back and climbing in.

I thought I saw something about not getting into a car with strangers... or talking to them, Ovi muttered.

They climbed in, and the driver sped off, the headlights barely lighting the road in front of them. Ovi looked like he was going to be ill and leaned his head out of the window. The driver glanced at them in the rearview mirror.

"Where are your parents?" he asked. "Are you kids supposed to be alone?"

"We were camping," Zara said without missing a beat. "They let us go alone all the time."

"Without any gear?" the man said, eyeing their small bags.

"Of course," Zara said. "We learned survival skills. How else are we supposed to test them?" The man chuckled at that and shrugged. The rest of the ride was silent, and he looked at them once in a while. The trip to Moshi was another twenty minutes, and the small, bustling town came into view. It looked much smaller at night without the chaos of daytime. The man dropped them off on a corner in the center of town. Zara thanked him. He shrugged one more time and left.

We should find some warmer clothes, Binita said, rubbing her arms. The night air was cool but barely. There were many shops and small stores around, but most were closed at this time of night. They had to wander around to find a hole-in-the-wall tourist shop that was staffed by a single man this late. Between the keychains, snacks, and necklaces, they found a few racks of long pants and a few thin sweatshirts. The girls grabbed some warm hats as well but were looking around for something warmer.

Do we really need all this? Kareem asked.

Yes, the girls said in unison, turning to him. The man at the front gave them an odd look. Kareem forgot he couldn't hear their conversations and probably thought they were making faces at each other without reason.

After grabbing the clothes and a few other supplies, they paid and left the store to search for Bahati's house. They weren't entirely sure where they were, and things didn't look as familiar at night as they did during the day. Ovi and Binita worked on reading the signs that they could find, and half an hour later, they were walking up to Bahati's door.

The four of them stood there in silence, none of them moving. *Should we, um, knock or something?* Binita asked.

Go ahead, Ovi said, backing away from the door.

Kareem should do it since he's team leader, Zara declared, folding her arms.

Fine, he said, squaring his shoulders and stepping up. He knocked three times, wincing at the noise it made. To be fair, who would want to be woken in the middle of the night?

Proving his point, they heard quick footsteps moving through the house, and the door was wrenched inward. Bahati stood before them, looking ready to commit a murder. "Aye!" she snapped. "Do you know what time it is!? My children are sleeping, and more kids are standing outside of my house asking for what? Hm?"

Kareem didn't dare point out that her yelling wasn't going to make matters any better. He cleared his through and started to apologize in her language, but he stumbled over the words, and the woman's face became more irritated. Just when she inhaled a breath to speak, Zara poked her head around Kareem and greeted the woman with a smile.

Kareem, Ovi, and Binita's mouths fell open as Bahati's anger melted upon seeing Zara's face. "My beautiful dear!" she cried, pulling her in. "It's so good to see you. How have you been? Such a wonderful girl."

Zara spoke to her, and the other three found themselves in an alternate reality as they were led through Bahati's house to the room with the portal. She asked Zara where they were headed, and she told them Toronto. She then went about setting up the crystals in parallel lines across the room. Kareem tried to catch Zara's eye, but her superior nose held resolutely forward.

The shimmering curtain of air suddenly rippled to life, and Bahati was ushering them through, saying goodbye to Zara and asking her to visit again. Kareem stepped through first and was immediately confused. It was much lighter, closer to sunset, but before him was a wall that looked out onto... clouds? The other three stepped through behind him, and he heard their gasps. Kareem tried to make sense of what he was looking at. The clouds moved, and then he saw it.

He had seen pictures of massive human cities with skyscrapers and steel and tar everywhere. He knew it was possible to be hundreds of feet in the air, but it was nothing like actually being there. Outside, the sun set on what he assumed was the city of Toronto to the left and what looked like an ocean on the right. The ground seemed miles away as he crept forward to look down. Behind him, he heard Ovi retching.

"First time?" a voice said in English, and Kareem turned to find a man expertly kicking a bucket in Ovi's direction just as he emptied the contents of his stomach. The man was skinny and had on a plush white robe as he lounged against the wall. His short hair was dyed blond and stood messily at all angles. Square glasses sat on his nose and reflected the light from his phone that he was scrolling through.

"Yes," Kareem said. "In a skyscraper, I mean."

"It gets boring," the man said. "My name is Adam. The door is through the hall." He pointed aimlessly behind him without looking up.

"Thanks," Kareem said and headed out. Binita rubbed Ovi's back and pushed him out behind Zara. They didn't have time to ogle the apartment, and Adam didn't seem interested in having four teenagers for guests. For all Kareem knew, venari came in and out of his home every day. He probably never had any privacy.

They went out into the hall and a short way away to find an elevator. Kareem pushed the down arrow and waited. The doors opened, and they stepped inside, and then nothing happened. The four of them stared and the massive panel of buttons.

Um, I'm not sure what to push. 1? Kareem said. Their classes hadn't gotten this specific. He knew very well what an elevator was but had no idea how to operate one.

There are several 1s, Zara said.

What about a letter? Binita said. *There's a G and a B. What do those even mean? Or there's the big red button.* She reached out her hand that Zara slapped away.

Kareem decided to push all of the lower numbers and the letters for safe measure. When the elevator shot down, they all yelped, grabbing onto the railings. It was one of the many things they had been told about in their human studies lessons, but feeling like you are falling hundreds of feet to the ground in a metal bottle would make anyone break out in a sweat.

The door stopped halfway down, and a woman with a large purse stepped inside, scanning them before reaching out to the panel. When she saw all the lower buttons pushed, she let out an "Oh" and stepped back to wait. The silence was long and awkward as they descended to the lower floors.

The elevators stopped too many times without anyone getting off before the ground floor came into view. The woman moved to step off first but turned to them. "You really shouldn't ride the elevator," she said with motherly disappointment and walked off into the lobby. The four of them followed her tentatively out into the lobby of the building. It had high ceilings and glossy floors that led to a set of glass doors to the street. It looked much darker down on the ground, and Kareem saw why as he pushed through the doors to go outside. All around him were more steel towers like he had seen in pictures. Although, most pictures of human cities showed the view of the skyline and not of the street. Like great, cold trees, the buildings blocked the setting sun, casting wide shadows on the people and the traffic that buzzed down below.

Next to him, Ovi inhaled a gasp. "It's so cold!" he said, wrapping his arms around himself. Zara and Binita shared a look, but they, too, were rubbing their arms. The thin sweaters they had grabbed were nowhere near enough, and Kareem quickly found the chilled air seeping in through the weave of his shirt, under the cuffs of his pants, and nipping at his ears.

"Let's hurry and find a hotel before we do anything else," Kareem said, pulling his sleeves over his fingers. Thankfully the buildings dampened the wind, but the air was still too cold for his liking.

The others agreed without protest, and they headed left down the street. Traffic was filtering out of the city for the evening, and the sidewalks were filled with people headed to dinner or home for the night. Kareem kept his eyes up, looking for a sign that advertised accommodation. They passed businesses and nondescript glass buildings and eventually came to a street lined with bright shops, clothing, and jewelry on display in the massive front windows. He didn't need to see the tags to know they were in an expensive area.

"That's it. I'm not going to freeze to death," Zara said suddenly.

Amid the protests of the others, she stormed over to the nearest shop and yanked the door open. Kareem muttered to himself and followed her inside with Ovi and Binita trailing behind him. Zara had already crossed half the store looking through the sparse racks. The place looked nearly out of business, with only a few items hung up here and there, yet three clerks stood at the back of the shop by the register, watching them like hawks. There was only one other woman in there, so it was hard to miss four ill-dressed teenagers.

Zara didn't seem to notice the clerks and was zipping around, picking up items and setting them down after feeling the fabric. "They really don't have much, do they?" Zara mumbled as she flicked through the racks while Kareem and the other two trailed behind her, not sure what to do. Eventually, she settled on a pale blue, puffy jacket and forced them to pick out something as well. Kareem tried not to make eye contact with one of the clerks who was watching them out of the corner of her eye, pretending to adjust one of the racks. Unease started to bubble in his stomach.

Zara collected their items and strode to the register, dumping them on the counter. The older clerk pursed her lips and said, "Find everything okay?" in a tone that dripped with condescension.

"Yes," Zara said in a satisfied huff. "And we won't be needing bags."

"Mhm." The clerk tapped on the screen and scanned the items, not bothering to take them off the hangers. "That'll be two thousand four hundred sixty-five dollars and forty cents," she said, still holding one of the jackets in her hand. They had no idea how much that was, but he had a sinking suspicion that four teenagers shouldn't be able to afford that.

Zara produced one of the fake credit cards Binita had stolen from a venari. The clerk took the card, eyes narrowing at them. "Did you kids steal this?"

Kareem stood behind Zara and didn't need to see her face to know her eyes narrowed to match the clerk's. "My father lets me have whatever I want," she said without missing a beat. She crossed her arms.

Creator! She's a good liar, Kareem thought.

The clerk flicked her eyebrows and swiped the card. "I can see that," she said under her breath. She handed back the card and slid the jackets across the counter, Binita snatching them up. "Have a good day."

Kareem couldn't get out of there fast enough, exhaling in relief when they got back out into the freezing cold air. He slipped his arms into the heavy black jacket and stuffed his hands into the packets.

"I could be wrong," Ovi said, sliding into his own coat, "but I think we're supposed to be *in*conspicuous."

Zara turned him a glare. "No point in being inconspicuous if we're dead," she said.

Before another retort could be hurled, Kareem cut in. "We really need to find a place to stay now." It was getting darker by the minute, and while he doubted the modern city would ever be completely without light, he knew it would be harder to find a place if they waited.

They set off down the street again, much warmer now. The fragments of sky above them were tinged pink with the setting sun, and stars dotted the far edges. They walked for nearly half an hour, getting away from what Kareem assumed was the dead center of downtown toward a livelier area with glitzy signs and flashing lights. The foot traffic had thinned and now swelled again with an abundance of restaurants and bars, the smells of food wafting out to the street. Binita groaned, eyeing the nearest restaurant with longing.

"We are never going to find Neelan in this mess," Ovi said suddenly.

They turned to him as they walked. "Not with that attitude, we won't," Zara shot back.

Kareem just kept going, keeping his eyes ahead of them. He wouldn't say it out loud, but he had been feeling the same. Each building had hundreds of rooms, and there were thousands of buildings just in the city alone. That was assuming that Neelan was here at all. How were they supposed to find him in all this? Honestly, who found *anything* in a massive city like this?

"I could really use some to eat," Binita said after they passed their fifth sign indicating hot sandwiches inside. "It's been days since I've had anything."

"We don't have time for that!" Zara said.

Kareem kept walking as Binita and Zara started bickering, but when Ovi jumped in to defend Binita, Kareem's patience wore thin. He spun around to face them. "That's enough!" They went quiet, glaring away from each other. Kareem sighed and looked around, catching sight of a small red sign across the street he had missed. It sat above a dirty brick building that looked as if it had missed more than a few repairs over the last few decades. He couldn't make out the swirling script of the sign, but he was pretty sure one of the words was "hotel."

"Okay, here's what we are going to do," he said. "Binita and Ovi, you two go get food. Zara and I will get rooms at that place over there." He pointed across the street at the sign. "Meet us there when you're done. And *please* blend in."

Binita and Ovi hurried away with little more than a backward glance. Kareem and Zara headed across the street to the building. It was an old building, several stories high, wedged between two other buildings. They went inside, and Zara immediately wrinkled her nose. A musty odor filled Kareem's nostrils, and the fluorescent lights were too bright. There was no one in line, and a skinny man with a goatee sat behind the counter, absentmindedly shuffling things around his desk.

Zara did the talking, asking for two rooms. The man looked them both over, asking them both for IDs. They handed them over, and Kareem's heart did a little flip-flop when he glanced at them over the little plastic cards. He was told the IDs were as good as real ones, but he hated to be scrutinized. It was pushing it to declare themselves of legal age, but the hotel didn't look like it could afford to turn away guests.

The man pursed his lips and handed the IDs back, along with two room keys, and instructed them to head up the elevator at the end of the hall. Before they went up, they told him their friends would be arriving soon and to send them to their room.

"Uh-huh," the man said.

The elevator looked like a death trap, so they took the stairs to the fifth floor and into one of the rooms that sat side-by-side. The rooms had the same musty scent and worn furniture. Old but plush chairs sat by the windows, and two beds were filled with mounds of lumpy pillows. Zara inspected the bathroom while Kareem looked out one of the windows that overlooked the street.

Night had fallen now, and he could no longer make out any of the pink in the sliver of sky above them. Down below, cars still zipped back and forth, and lights flashed near the entrances of the buildings. At eye level across the street, rows upon rows of windows stared back and him. From the vantage point in Adam's apartment, the city looked huge, even bigger than Rhapta. Where was Neelan in all of that? Where was the ubir? They had so little to go on, and now that they were here, Kareem had a sinking feeling it would all be for nothing. It almost seemed foolish how confident they had all been back on the venari rooftop, going over their plan to find and return Neelan. They were just pupils, having barely trained for a few months. Why did they ever think they would be better at finding a missing Anunnaki than venari, who had been training for decades?

"We'll find him, you know," Zara said from behind him,

making him jump a little. He turned to find her sitting sideways in one of the plush chairs, her hair hanging over the armrest. She said it so matter-of-factly that his brow immediately wrinkled.

"How do you know?" he asked. "All we've done is bicker since we got here."

She sighed. "You were right," she said, ignoring his question. "We all have our roles to play, and I'm finding that mine is to pull that big head of yours back into reality." Kareem opened his mouth to protest, but she was ready. "Haven't you noticed how far we've come? We were *deplorable* in our first few weeks of training. Like, terrible. But look at us now." She snagged a pamphlet off the side table next to her and started thumbing through it. "If we can do all that, then I think we can manage to find one venari."

Kareem realized she was right. Less than a few months ago, he had thought they would all be expelled from venari training. They went from being nearly hostile to each other to using each other's strengths to win the skirmish, sneak out of Rhapta, and travel across the planet without getting caught. If any of the other pupils knew where they were right now... well, they just wouldn't believe it.

Zara gave him a small smile over the edge of the booklet she held, a vast difference from the way she looked at him the day they met.

"Don't order any room service," was all he said, earning him a roll of her eyes.

Just then, the door opened, and in walked far too many packages of food and a beaming Binita, Ovi closing the door behind her. Now they just needed to come up with their next plan.

CHAPTER 18

FINDING THE LOST

The sounds of the city woke them early. They were somehow the same sounds and totally different from the ones Kareem had heard in Jaipur. Shouts and honking, and electronic wails came from outside the window. He could hear the girls moving around in the next room, and Ovi was tossing in the bed next to him. Kareem padded over to Ovi and shook his shoulder.

What? he said, not bothering to speak out loud.

"Time to go," Kareem said, heading for the bathroom. He heard Ovi's groan as he shut the door.

Within ten minutes, all four of them were back out on the street in the early morning cold.

"Where do we even start?" Binita said, looking around at the traffic.

Kareem had thought about this all night, tossing and turning in bed. Ubir slowly became more insane the longer they continued to perform the blood rite, but most were still coherent enough to know that getting caught by humans was a bad idea. So they tended to stay in dark corners and back alleys. The only information they had on the ubir that was in Toronto was a name: Adonal. None of them knew who that was or what kind of abilities he had. They didn't have time to question all of Rhapta to see who had known him.

After relaying this information to his team, Kareem and the others just started walking. The sun rose slowly, sending some streets in a blaze of light while leaving others in the shadowed dark. They walked the alleys between buildings, traipsed through rougher areas with homeless people huddled against the cold, and through sunny parks. It still hadn't snowed yet, and people flocked to greener areas despite the chilly air. Kareem grew warm inside his jacket after hours of walking. Binita tried to ask a few locals some questions, but they were received very differently from how Neelan had in Jaipur. People vehemently shook their heads when Binita walked up to them, but most flat-out ignored her, like she wasn't even there.

"So much for 'Canada nice,'" Binita muttered after her fourth try.

"What exactly are we going to do when we find Adonal?" Ovi asked. They were seated on a bench at the edge of a small park, watching people walk by, none of which looked even the slightest like an ubir.

Kareem hadn't actually thought that far. "Um, I suppose we would need to question him, assuming he doesn't have Neelan with him."

Zara shivered. "What if Neelan's dead?"

"He won't be," Ovi snapped. "We'll find him."

"I'm not saying we won't, but we have no idea the state he'll be in when we do," Zara replied. She had her chin dipped inside the collar of her jacket.

"The only option is to capture the ubir, tie him up, and hope he's sane enough to answer our questions," Binita said. She was digging in the dead grass behind the bench and, finding nothing, sat on the bench next to Zara.

Kareem looked around at the city that surrounded them. The park behind them, the streets on both sides, and the vastness of Lake Ontario peeked between the buildings in front of them. *If I were ubir, where would I go?* Kareem thought to himself. Where in the city would be away from prying eyes? The blood rite was essentially a sacrifice the ubir had to make, and it would need to be done where pedestrians wouldn't be strolling by. Kareem shuddered at the thought. His eyes roved over the area again, catching on the glint of the lake when a thought struck him.

"It *smells*," Zara said, covering her nose with her sleeve.

Kareem was inclined to agree, but he hadn't expected anything less when they crept onto the wharf on the Northwest side of the city. Barges docked further down, and the area was like a small city in itself, filled with warehouses and shipping containers. Workers unloaded a nearby boat, not paying attention to the four teenagers slinking between the low warehouses.

"It wouldn't be difficult to hide a body around here, though," Ovi added, "with the smell and all. A good place for ubir." The others nodded in agreement.

They moved away from the workers, weaving around the warehouses and containers. Some were unlocked, and when they looked inside, they were basically empty. They quickly checked each one, but far more were locked that they didn't bother breaking into. The day was wearing on, and they weren't any closer to finding Neelan than when they started. Regardless of whether or not they did, they would need to leave by tomorrow night at the latest to be back in time for lessons the following day.

Kareem hadn't even begun to think about how they were going to sneak back into the city without being seen by any of the guards. *Probably the same way we left,* he supposed.

Three-quarters of the way up the wharf, they found a rather run-down warehouse that wasn't too large. The rusted door banged against the siding when they went in. There was one large room with a second mezzanine level at the back. Old blankets lay crammed in a few of the corners, with empty bags of food and garbage scattered here and there. A few empty crates sat in a corner, and some supplies hung against one wall, but most were old-looking and worn. It could have easily been a shelter for ubir and human alike, yet they found no indication that anyone had been there recently, so they left.

Back outside, the only sounds were of the water lapping against the side of the wharf and a few seagulls scavenging for trash. They were far from the bustle of the downtown traffic, and there were no workers around either, yet they hadn't found a single clue pointing them in the direction of the ubir. The sun was on its downward arc again and would set soon. They had been here a full day, and nothing had come of it. Kareem's jaw ached from how hard he clenched it.

"Let's split up for a bit so we can finish searching these last few warehouses. After that, we might as well head back," he said with a sigh.

The others just nodded, looking as dejected as he felt. They were cold, far from home, and unaccomplished. Kareem couldn't blame them for their lack of enthusiasm. They separated to go through the last remaining rows of the wharf, and Kareem started peeking into the nearest warehouse. It was just as empty as the others, so he continued out, listening for the others' footsteps and the opening and closing of the doors, making sure they stayed close.

He had made it through the third row of buildings when a

sharp cry pierced the air. It was short, the sound carrying up at the end like the owner was confused, not aware that they were even crying out.

"Zara?" Kareem called, jogging toward the sound. "Ovi?"

"Kareem!" Ovi shouted.

He was at full speed now, running around the warehouses toward Ovi's voice. He shouted for them and saw a flash of Ovi's dark green jacket, and a second later, he heard the growl of a man. He heard footsteps behind him and stole a glance back to see Zara's feet pounding on the concrete after him toward the sound of the cry. He came to a section of shipping containers stacked at the end of the wharf, turning the corner where he saw Ovi's jacket disappear. Just as he did, Binita's scream rented the air.

In the narrow alley of containers, Ovi was swinging a short piece of metal at a man who looked beyond the realm of sanity. Just like the ubir in Jaipur, this one had wild eyes and erratic movements, lurching and jerking away from Ovi while viscously trying to grab at the piece of metal. His hair had been left to grow out unevenly, and his clothes hung off a body that hadn't seen soap in a good long while. Binita was using the side of a container to regain her footing and ran toward the ubir to help Ovi.

Kareem dashed forward to help, but the ubir saw him and Zara, and immediately a second set of razor-sharp teeth descended down over his real ones in a snarl. Like a cornered dog, the ubir swiped at them madly while baring his teeth. He was trying to back away from their group, but Zara had snuck around the other side and was closing him in.

Kareem ran between Ovi and Binita, reaching to make contact with the ubir. The ubir moved much faster than he anticipated and backhanded Kareem hard enough that zaps of light crossed his vision as he stumbled. He heard the others yell out, and the ubir went ballistic, lashing at them faster than they could control. Kareem awkwardly scrambled toward the ubir to grab his ankle, tripping over his own hands and knees in the process. He barely touched the ubir's leg, but it was barely enough to stick his foot to the ground, making him topple sideways, although he maintained his footing.

Everything was happening so fast, and Kareem felt out of control. Ovi had backed away against the far container, but Zara, in all her rage, had come close and sent her fist at the ubir's face. He twisted quickly, and her knuckles still clipped his ear, but it was as if he didn't even feel it. Now that Zara was close, the ubir grabbed her so fast that Kareem hardly even saw it. Before he could register what was happening, the ubir's head came down, and razor-sharp teeth, like those of a shark, sank deep into Zara's shoulder, where her jacket had slipped back.

The blood came almost as fast as Zara's scream. She tried to wrench away, but the ubir held tight. Panic flooded Kareem's veins, and he grabbed the ubir's arm, yanking back just as Binita latched onto the ubir's head to pull him from Zara. All of a sudden, the entire mass of them lurched as the ubir's foot came unstuck, throwing Kareem to the ground and releasing Zara, who fell back.

Binita was still clinging to the ubir whose hand scrabbled against her to find purchase. He grabbed the back of her jacket, yanking her back just enough. Grabbing a fistful of her hair, he pulled her head to the side at an angle, exposing her neck.

Time seemed to slow, and Kareem's blood chilled in his veins as he realized what the ubir intended to do.

Binita was going to die.

Bloodied teeth shot out, but suddenly a choked cry came suddenly from the other side of the ubir, and a halting gasp came violently from the man. He dropped Binita to the ground, where she stayed in shock. Kareem saw on the other side of the ubir Ovi had bare hands wrapped around his arm and neck. The ubir's eyes had gone wide, and he stood shaking and frozen in the same position, the breath coming in quick, broken gasps until his eyes rolled back in his head and his teeth slammed together.

Kareem watched as the paralyzed ubir fell to the ground, nearly stiff as a board, leaving Ovi, chest heaving, standing above him.

The ubir didn't move. Unlike when Kareem had been shocked by Caden, the paralysis didn't end, and based on the broken breaths coming out of him, Kareem wasn't sure he would live. He blinked, looking around at the situation through a haze of adrenaline and shock.

Binita sat on the ground, huddled in on herself and unmoving. Ovi still stood above the ubir but held his hands away from himself as if he were afraid of harming himself. It was Zara's own breathing that brought Kareem back into the moment. Blood soaked her jacket, and she was struggling to get to her feet.

There were no humans around, but they had been making plenty of noise. Who knew if the worker from down the wharf had strayed this way? There was also no telling if Ovi's ability would wear off or if they were about to have a body on their hands within minutes. Kareem needed to come up with a plan quickly.

KAREEM STRUGGLED under the weight of the ubir. The man wasn't huge, but Ovi and Binita struggled on his other side, half dragging him back through the wharf. Zara hurried ahead of them, one hand clutching at her shoulder. Thanks to the Anunnaki healing, the bleeding had stopped, but she would need to rest soon. Kareem didn't know how she had the energy to stand.

"Here!" she said, moving to one of the small warehouses on the left. The one they had seen earlier was both unlocked and empty. Kareem helped drag the ubir inside, dropping him in the middle of the room. The three of them got to work searching for some sort of bindings in the garbage that lay jumbled in the corners of the large room while Zara sat with her back against the wall, wincing.

They all appeared in various states of shock. Nothing about this was like their training. It was uncoordinated and messy, and Kareem felt like he was barely hanging onto any semblance of control of the events. The sun was on its last legs and sent beams of light at an angle through the high windows. They found some worn rope and a couple of plastic strips they used to tie the ubir's hands behind his back, leaving him in the middle of the room. Now that he had stopped snarling, Kareem could see he was much younger than he had originally thought, maybe in his midtwenties at best. How could someone so young choose this life?

"How long until he wakes up?" Zara asked as Ovi came over to look at her shoulder.

He shrugged. "No idea if he even will."

"So we wait," Kareem said, leaning against a wall. Binita came and sat next to him, her eyes wide but not saying anything.

They stayed there for nearly an hour, watching the light move across the room and disappear completely before another long gasp came from the ubir. His limbs shuddered and folded into himself before he groaned and tried to sit up. Upon realizing he was bound, he gave a delirious snarl and started thrashing.

"You won't be able to remove those, so I wouldn't bother trying," Kareem said as he watched him struggle.

The ubir's eyes were wild and roving as he sat up and saw them. They were so like the other ubir in Jaipur. The same erratic movements and unfocused gaze, like he was slipping in and out of some drug-induced state. This was not at all how Kareem imagined being a venari would be like. Just months ago, he imagined himself traveling the world and returning bravely to Rhapta with an ubir bound and to the proud faces of his people. They stood there, in a cold warehouse in the dark, bleeding, exhausted, and near hopeless in finding their mentor. Reality had dealt them a grim hand.

Kareem opened his mouth to speak, but Zara cut in.

"Why did you do it?" she said, her voice loud and clear despite the pain she must've been in. "Why did you become ubir?" It wasn't what they were here for, but the others stayed silent, waiting for an answer.

The ubir chuckled, the sound odd to Kareem's ears. "Just children..." his voice came quietly before trailing off. "I pity you," he said louder, his voice cracking from disuse.

The group was quiet, and he kept talking. "We are animals to Rhapta," he snarled, whipping his head around to look at them. "Chained, caged... We cannot leave." He said nothing more.

Ovi's brow furrowed. "That's not true," he said. "The new laws—"

The ubir barked a laugh, loud and sharp this time. "You think they don't have ways to control you?" he asked. His eyes continued to roam while his speech became semi-coherent with his anger.

Kareem, worried that they would lose any sanity he had, cut in. "This isn't why we captured you," he said, stepping forward. "There was a venari that came through Toronto several weeks ago. His name is Neelan, green eyes—"

The ubir choked on a laugh. "Yes, yes," he said deliriously as he rocked to the side, "pretty spring green eyes..."

Kareem and the group straightened. He had seen Neelan! "Where is he?" he demanded, stepping forward.

"Gone."

The group went still. "What do you mean gone?" Kareem demanded again, his voice dropping low.

"Dead," the ubir said, tilting his head as if listening to something. His teeth had retracted, and he was smacking his mouth together.

A quiet sob escaped from Binita, tears spilling down her cheeks from where she sat, but no one else said anything. Neelan could not be dead; Kareem refused to believe it.

"What do you mean?" Kareem asked, his voice rising. He barely registered the tension in his arms as he clenched his fists.

The ubir just shrugged, and Kareem wanted to pummel him, but the ubir's face changed suddenly. He looked sad, as if he just remembered some deep-rooted pain. "Everything hurts," he mumbled quietly. "Everything always—"

"Did you do something with him?" Kareem asked louder. His anger was rising, and he wanted to rip the answers from the ubir. Neelan could not be dead, but if he was, he wanted to know exactly what the ubir did before Kareem killed him. He thought about Neelan sitting in his room playing the mbira. He never told Kareem why a musician would so desperately want to become venari, and he would never find out.

"Yes." The nonchalant tone made him sick.

"Where is he now? Where is his body?" Kareem asked.

"I don't know. Everything hurts..."

"Why did you do it then?" Binita suddenly snapped. "*Why?*" she asked through her tears.

"I didn't know it would be like this!" the ubir shouted, looking back at them. He was breathing hard, and Kareem couldn't help but realize he had just thought the same thing moments ago. The ubir was probably only a few years older than Tejas and had a name once; Adonal. But Kareem couldn't think of him as a person right now. All he could think about was him killing Neelan and leaving his body somewhere to rot.

"There are healers—" Ovi started.

"I won't go back!" the ubir shouted. "It's too late," he said quieter.

Zara snorted. "So you decided to become a murderer instead of dealing with whatever problems you had in the city."

"Not a murderer," the ubir said, shaking his head slowly while looking at the ground. The makeshift bindings pinned his arms back, and his chin dipped to his chest. "I only take the ones... I'm given..." His head tilted back, and his eyes roamed the ceiling high above them. He was rocking back and forth, becoming more delirious by the second. Ubir needed to complete the blood rite at regular intervals. The drug addicts, they needed it less at first, but the more they did it, the more they needed it, or they would descend into madness. How long had it been since he had last performed the rite?

"Given?" Ovi said. Kareem didn't care. He just wanted to know where Neelan's body was so they could bring him home. "What does that mean?"

"By the people..."

That caught Kareem's attention. "People? What people?" He and the others were watching the ubir intently, but he had closed his eyes and just rocked.

Suddenly his eyes flew wide, and his head swiveled to the windows, looking.

"Just tell us!" Zara yelled, getting to her feet. The fact that the temperature in the room had remained unchanging was a testament to how injured she was.

The ubir ignored them and continued to watch the windows.

"Tell us, and we'll let you go," Kareem offered. Ovi and Binita's heads whipped toward him, but they stayed quiet.

"A group of people," the ubir said finally.

"You said that," Kareem growled. "*What* people?"

It was silent for a while. The only sound was the ubir's rocking back and forth, his clothes swishing. Finally, his eyes roamed in their direction again. "They offered a deal," he said, and Kareem's chest grew tight. "I bring them Anunnaki, and they give me sacrifices for the rite."

He stopped rocking, but for all Kareem knew, the warehouse was spinning around him.

In their silence, the ubir spoke again. "They're bad people, though, the ones they bring me. No innocents…"

The others were rooted to their spot, looking like they were trying to process what the ubir had said as much as Kareem was. There were people that wanted Anunnaki? Who even knew about them? Were they behind the Anunnaki disappearances? What was going on?

"What?!" Zara said for all of them finally.

"Who are these people?" Kareem said, stalking forward, just feet from the ubir.

The ubir only shrugged. His eyes were wandering again, a sign of his madness creeping back in. He rocked back and forth, shaking his head. "Never said… I've seen letters…" He shuddered suddenly, as if remembering. "SPE."

Zara glanced at Kareem, and he could only shake his head. He was just as confused as they were.

"So these people," Binita said tentatively, "they have Neelan?"

"Yes." The word brought both hope and terror into Kareem in equal measure. Neelan was alive, but was that any better? What were these people doing with him? Kareem's mind was whirling. Did Rhapta know about this? Did the queen? There were too many questions and too many possibilities. He needed to find a way to get Neelan or get help. In the storm of his thoughts, something dawned on him.

"When are you supposed to see them again? These people; SPE?"

The ubir rocked violently back and forth, throwing his head around. "Hours… ago…" he spat out.

Kareem and the others shared a look but a sound cut through the night. The sound of a van door being slammed shut.

The ubir stopped rocking. The group stopped breathing. Footsteps, several of them, marched outside. Kareem glanced back at the door they had come in. It was unlocked and sat like a flimsy barrier between them and whoever was outside.

A snapping sound and Zara's yelp had Kareem turning back to find the ubir dashing across the warehouse, his bindings in a shredded heap where he had sat. Razor-sharp claws of bone protruded from the ubir's hands as he jumped and crashed through a nearby window, and the footsteps came around that side of the building as well. There was a struggling sound, and Kareem had no idea if it was the ubir or whoever was out there.

Kareem! Ovi warned inside his head, but Kareem was already running toward the back of the room. He had no idea what was happening, but he knew it would be very bad if they were caught. They couldn't go out the way they came in, nor through the window the ubir had jumped through. There was another door at the back behind a crate, but Kareem wasn't surprised to find the door firmly locked when he yanked on the handle.

Who is that?! Binita said, looking back at the opposite door.

Doesn't matter, Zara said, running over with a crowbar she found along the wall. *We need to go!* She started wedging it in the crack between the door in the frame while Kareem pulled at the handle. The lock was weak and bending, but not quickly enough. Suddenly the opposite door clanged open, slamming against the wall. Two men in pale blue uniforms stalked inside, carrying something small and sharp in one hand. Kareem could make out a small circular logo on the upper left side of their clothes, but he couldn't read it in the dim light. They could see more uniformed people behind them and the edge of a white van outside.

Hurry! Binita shrieked into their minds.

Heart hammering in his chest, Kareem used his ability to lock his hands onto the handle and pulled, shoving Zara out of the way in the process. The frame whined and flung open with force, and the group shot out into the night, not looking behind them. There weren't as many of the uniformed group as they thought. Only one woman was coming around the side of the building carrying a small tablet in one hand and a flashlight in the other. She called out to her companions when she saw them, but Kareem urged them to run.

The sky was dark now. Tall floodlights were on near the edge of the wharf by the boats, giving them just enough light to see by as they sprinted away from the warehouse and the blue-uniformed people. Kareem heard footsteps behind him but didn't dare turn to look, just running faster, zigzagging between more warehouses and containers, shooting for the tall buildings downtown, not far away. If they could just get into the city, they could lose them.

He was about to put on another burst of speed when he noticed only Ovi and Binita running before him. Zara was lagging behind; one arm tucked tight against her side. Kareem cursed himself for forgetting her injury despite the situation. She was probably in pain. He slowed just enough to grab the hand on her good side and pulled her forward faster, their breath coming in pants.

Head for downtown! Kareem said in their minds, not wanting their chasers to hear if they were close. He hadn't seen them behind Zara, but they could be close. Anunnaki were naturally faster than humans, but that only went so far. If what the ubir said was true, these people would go to great lengths to capture them. But Kareem calculated the chances of them publicly kidnapping a group of teenagers on a busy downtown street were low.

None of them looked back again, nor did they slow until they were back near the shopping area they had been to the night before. The area was full of people out in the early evening, and they had to slow to a jog to avoid a collision. They earned a few glares from pedestrians. A few of them noticed the blood on Zara's jacket, and their heads swiveled to look as they hurried by. Two people even tried to stop them and ask if they were okay, but they didn't answer them and just kept going. Kareem really hoped they wouldn't call the police.

Finally, Kareem chanced a look around them, and he didn't see any of the pale blue uniforms, so he let his team stop their mad run. They still whipped their heads around them and kept their eyes glued up just in case.

I think we are safe for the moment, Ovi said while he panted.

Kareem wasn't so sure, but they decided to leave their bags at the hotel and headed straight for Adam's apartment. As they got close, Kareem halted so fast, Binita ran face-first into his back. Peeking around his shoulder, the rest of them saw why and immediately backpedaled the way they came.

A white van with a circular logo sat further down the street. This time they could make out the faint stylized logo painted nondescriptly on the door: SPE.

Kareem could hardly think straight, his thought in a panicked jumble in his mind, and they hurried down the street, looking over their shoulders as they went. He didn't know what to do and was still reeling over what they had discovered.

The Anunnaki weren't running away, and ubir weren't killing them. They were being captured.

By humans.

This was bad. *Bad, bad, bad.*

They were way in over their heads, and Kareem desperately wished that Tejas were here with him. Or Hessa, or Amol, or even Laban, if he was going to admit how desperate he was. But in the end, it was just him and his team.

Without a word, they crept several blocks out of the way before slowly making it back to the hotel. They waited down the street for nearly twenty minutes before going inside. Kareem peeked into the lobby at the counter. He didn't see anyone but heard a voice coming from an open room to the right of the counter, possibly a break room for the staff. He motioned for the others to hurry, and they headed straight for the stairs to their floor, all piling into one room and locking the door tightly. Ovi and Kareem pushed a desk and two chairs against the door as well for good measure.

Binita immediately curled up into the center of one of the beds while Ovi looked at Zara's shoulder. The bite marks had all healed over, but she looked weak and winced when Ovi poked her shoulder. But she was so tired, and as soon as Ovi stepped away, her eyelids drooped down, and she fell asleep in one of the armchairs by the window. Neither Ovi nor Kareem spoke. They just sat there, attempting to process all that had happened in the last few hours. After far too long of trying to sort through the mess in his head, Kareem walked over to the remaining bed and passed out on top of the blankets.

CHAPTER 19

RAMIFICATIONS

They stayed inside all day, barely saying a word. They kept the shades down, peeking down at the street every now and again to look for signs of white vans or those pale blue uniforms. It wasn't until late morning that they figured those people, SPE, didn't know where they were. Not wanting to risk it, they planned to wait until the afternoon before leaving.

The four of them began to pack up their things as the day wore on. As they were quietly gathering their items, Zara suddenly spoke. *So are we just going to leave Neelan?*

What else are we supposed to do? Ovi said. *We don't even know where he is.*

Binita zipped her bag and sat up. *I'm not even sure I understand entirely what is going on. Who are those people, and what do they want with us?*

Silence followed. They had all been thinking the same thing, and none of them had answers.

No idea, Zara said, *but they have to be bad if they are kidnapping Anunnaki and employing ubir to do it.*

What happened to the ubir, by the way? Ovi said from his spot on the floor. *Do you guys see the claws that came out of him? I'm pretty sure they were bone.*

Ovi and Zara continued talking, but Kareem watched Binita's face. She was deep in thought, staring at the closed window, when she suddenly stood up and headed for the door. *I'll be right back,* she said to Kareem.

It doesn't matter what happened to the ubir at this point, Zara said, tucking her feet underneath her on one of the beds. She was looking much better than the day before, a little light coming back into her face. *We need to get back to the city as soon as possible.*

Ovi nodded. *Yeah, the best bet is to talk to someone there. Maybe the queen can help!*

Zara jumped up. *Absolutely not! We have to keep this a secret. Right, Kareem?* She didn't bother waiting for his answer and continued to spark an argument with Ovi. Kareem dozed against a wall for what felt like hours, but it must have only been a few minutes before Binita stepped back into the room.

Where did you go? Ovi asked her.

To that little computer room we saw down in the lobby the other day, she said. In her hands was a stack of paper. *I just did a quick search of SPE and printed off all the pages I could find so we could take them with us.*

Kareem and the others gathered over her papers as she spoke. *I honestly didn't find much, but I didn't spend a lot of time searching. SPE comes up as a research organization that does medical testing and a few other little things. There are a few subsidiaries, but that's it; nothing special.* She shrugged.

Where are they located? Kareem asked. He was pretty sure the Anunnaki that had gone missing were not from the same place.

There are headquarters all over the world, but the addresses were hard to find, and nothing seemed too definite. There just wasn't a lot of information, Binita said.

I can see that, Ovi added, looking over the pages Binita had printed off.

Kareem sighed. This did nothing to help the maddening confusion in his head. He still didn't know what to do for Neelan, but they had to do something. *We can keep researching when we get back to Rhapta, but until then, we aren't safe. Also, Zara needs to see a healer sooner rather than later.*

I'm fine, she snapped, glaring at him with her icy eyes.

Kareem didn't give her the satisfaction of glaring back and said, *We'll decide what to do when we get home. Regardless of whether we tell anyone, we need to get out of this city and back to Rhapta.* The others nodded in agreement.

They left shortly after that, dropping the plastic keycard off at the front desk and inching out onto the street. It was a relatively quiet afternoon, and they didn't see any suspicious vehicles or anyone running after them, so they made their way to Adam's. Kareem made them wait a full ten minutes outside and down the street before considering the coast clear to head into the lobby. This time he punched only a single button on the elevator, and it shot up into the sky.

"Back so soon?" Adam said when he answered the door, hardly paying attention to them. He had on a form-fitting t-shirt and cotton shorts; the heat was cranked up inside the apartment, and Kareem's jacket was suddenly far too warm. They would need to discard the winter clothing in Moshi. It would be too risky trying to sneak it into the city.

Adam set up the crystals faster than he had seen anyone do it before. Despite his lack of enthusiasm, his work was precise and efficient. He was already walking out of the room by the time the group stepped across the portal.

In Bahati's house, the loud voices of children came from every direction, and soon enough, Bahati herself came into the room, gushing over Zara, who feigned delight. Seeing the Ummanu woman smile was almost the most shocking thing that had happened to Kareem in the last few days.

Almost.

One of these days, you're going to need to explain what kind of spell you put on her, Ovi said grimly into their minds. Zara only rolled her eyes at him.

They hurried out into the early late evening, glad that the sun was setting already. They wanted to sneak back into the city under cover of darkness, and it would take them several hours to get there. The unfortunate problem was getting a ride to the starting point. This late in the evening, there were no buses headed to the mountain, and none of them knew how to hotwire a car. They waited at the bus station for nearly forty minutes before they found someone willing to drive them out there for payment. The older man hardly glanced at them in the rearview mirror once, and twenty-five minutes later, they were at the base of the mountain, bags in hand, and watching the car retreat back to Moshi.

Zara heaved a sigh. *Let's get this over with,* she said.

The trek was miserable. It was starting to get rather cool on the way up without the sun's heat, but the mosquitos were just as vicious. They had one flashlight between them, and they slowly made their way up. They had to stop more than once to reorient themselves, but they still neared the entrance after a few hours. They were all quiet again, tired and dejected. There was no stake in the ground like most of the entrances had, but they felt the barrier tug gently at them as they passed through.

Kareem exhaled in relief. They were safe.

Two figures emerged from the trees with obsidian-tipped spears. Kareem didn't need light to know that red symbols were painted over their bodies. All warriors had them, as did the guards that patrolled the city. By the contemptuous expressions on their faces, it seemed they expected them to be here.

Ovi groaned, and Kareem was inclined to agree.

They had been caught.

FOR THE THIRD TIME, Kareem sat in Savar's office. In all of the years leading up to him becoming a venari pupil, not once had he expected to be in this position unless it was to be praised. Yet here he was, absolutely sure he was going to be expelled, for the third time.

He and his team were marched straight to the house of the venari. It was a blessing he wasn't sent directly to the Grand Hall or the dungeons under the city. As soon as they got inside, Hessa, Zaid, Amol, and Laban were all there, each taking a pupil. Zaid marched Kareem up the stairs to Savar's office and pushed him down into the chair he had come to dread before leaving to talk with Savar out in the hall. The fact that Zaid was here at all was bad. It meant that more than just the house of the venari knew they had left.

Kareem waited for several minutes. He was somehow both wide awake and tired to the bone. Finally, Savar stepped in and walked around his desk to sit in his chair. Kareem stared down at his lap for so long that he had to take a peek to see if Savar was still there.

He was, and he was staring right at him, a deep frown etched into his skin. *What were you doing in Canada?*

Kareem suddenly didn't want to tell Savar where exactly they had been. He wanted to talk with his team first. Putting on a puzzled face, he said, *We were in Moshi. The little town down at the—*

Savar's face melted into impatient irritation. *You do realize that the queen has a team of seers, yes? Even if they don't always understand their visions, they provide enough for us to figure out where four of our pupils went. They can't see everything, but they see enough, so stop lying.*

Kareem dropped his act, eyeing the older venari. The ubir Adonal had said something that weaseled its way back into his mind. Something about Rhapta's control...

I'm going to give you one chance to explain, Savar said, lacing his fingers together.

Kareem didn't have a choice then. His team would probably be undergoing similar treatment soon, and there was no way all four of them would be able to keep quiet. So he told him everything; Neelan disappearing, training to win the skirmish, the fight with the ubir and what he told them, and even about SPE. He glossed over the parts where they broke into his office on more than one occasion. By the time he finished, Kareem was absolutely positive he would be thrown in the dungeons. Saying his team's plan out loud made him sound nearly insane.

Savar's expression was stony; lips pressed together. He leaned back in disbelief, rolling his eyes to the ceiling. *I'm too old for this,* he bit out. *I'm sick of children and their antics.*

Kareem refused to feel ashamed. *We were just trying to find out what happened to Neelan,* he said, leaning forward.

Savar dropped his chin to look him in the eyes. *We already know about SPE.*

That was the last thing Kareem expected him to say. The words were like a punch in the gut. Kareem's face must've been a mixture of outrage and confusion because Savar leaned forward and continued.

SPE was loosely involved in the Battle of Rhapta five years ago. They never broke through the city's defenses, but we are aware that they know of us. We have no idea how much they know, but knowing at all is too much.

Kareem's mouth hung open like a fish. He eagerly leaned

forward. *So you're sending people to rescue Neelan and the other Anunnaki?*

Savar shook his head. *Unfortunately, there is nothing we can do at the moment. They are rather good at discretion, and we were sure they were unaware we knew of them. We were planning on using this in our favor, but that is no longer in the cards,* he said, eyeing Kareem distastefully. *We'll have to wait until they make another move.*

Tight anger claimed Kareem's muscles. Despite his weariness, he wanted to rally the warriors and all the venari and march against SPE at dawn. How could they do nothing knowing their people were in danger? And they didn't even tell anyone; the families of the missing would have no idea what happened.

So you knew what would happen to him, and you sent him anyway? Kareem snapped, his voice sharp and hot.

Neelan understood his job and the risks, Savar shot back. He hesitated a moment before saying, *Do you know why I chose you as the leader of your team, Kareem?*

Kareem just glared at him, not trusting himself to respond civilly.

Because you cared, Savar said, capturing his eyes and his voice rising. *More than the others, you wanted this and pushed for it. But that is also your biggest weakness. You want so badly to be venari that you are blinded by reality and its dangers. You could have died. Your teammates could have died.* Savar's scowl matched Kareem's own now. *You could have exposed us all!* he shouted, slamming a hand down on his desk.

There was nothing to say, so Kareem slid his angry gaze to his lap, and he heard Savar sigh.

Return to your room and await your punishment. Whether or not you are expelled will be decided shortly.

Kareem stood quickly, heading for the door.

Oh, Savar added, *but if you try to leave the city, you will be impris-*

oned without question, and there is nothing I can do to help you. His gaze when Kareem looked back was anything but gentle.

Kareem left Savar's office, having disappointed him for a third time.

CHAPTER 20
UNDER WATCHFUL EYES

The afternoon sun was as sweltering as it was every other day, but Kareem and his team found some relief beneath the trees. He, Zara, and Ovi lounged on the ground while Binita chucked stones into the stream a few feet away. Across the field, a figure in red paint strolled near the city gate. Every now and again, he would glance toward where they sat in the trees, but Kareem was sure he couldn't hear them.

They had been confined to their rooms for three days. On the fourth, they were released and, surprisingly, not expelled. That's not to say they came out unscathed. The list of menial tasks they had to complete extended for months, and they were placed on probation until further notice. It took Kareem a few days to realize there were additional stipulations to their probation, such as the warrior that was doing little to hide the fact that he and some of his brethren were tailing them wherever they went. With the extent of their punishments, they had very little time to leave the house of the venari, but when they did, there was always a nondescript warrior keeping just out of sight.

Is he still there? Ovi asked, flicking a leaf into the air.

Kareem nodded, leaning back against a tree. Their families hadn't been told what had happened. They would require the government to admit they knew about SPE, and Kareem and his team had been sworn into secrecy. He was almost 90 percent sure the only reason they were still allowed to train was so the venari could keep an eye on them. Those who knew had been livid, but Kareem didn't care.

They had resumed their training days ago, and only a few pupils had caught wind that *something* had happened on their days off. It took all of Kareem's will not to punch the twentieth person who tried asking him what happened. But they weren't his concern now. His team was his primary focus, and they needed him desperately, whether they realized it or now.

A splash had them turning their heads to Binita, who stood ankle-deep in the stream. She had tossed a larger rock out into the water, this time after running out of the little stones around her feet. She had been doing this quietly for nearly twenty minutes. In fact, she had been much more reclusive than normal, almost like how she was when they first met, disappearing and going off on her own, talking little when the group was together. Kareem refused to allow his team to lose the progress they'd made.

Ovi's eyes lingered a little longer on her back. Late the second night of their confinement, while the lights were out and they tried to sleep, he and Kareem had started talking into the dark. It was about nothing and everything at first, but then the conversation had turned to what he had done to the ubir. Kareem hadn't been able to see his face, but the other boy's voice had wavered a few times as he talked about his ability, about how it scared him. There had been a hint of a memory that was the root of Ovi's fear, but Kareem had learned not to push him. At least not yet. Ovi's ability had proved extraordinarily useful and subdued the ubir, and he needed to embrace it and control it.

Kareem glanced over at Zara, who stabbed at the dirt with a

stick, absentmindedly drawing circles. She had seen a healer right after they arrived back, and she was deemed healthy again soon after. Kareem had no intentions of holding back on pushing her. She just didn't know it yet. There had hardly been any time to talk from the moment they won the skirmish to now, but what she had done with her ability during the skirmish hung in the air between them. Tala, their abilities instructor, told Zara that she could do far more than she believed, and Kareem had seen proof of that. Whatever she had done had created such force that an entire room full of venari and pupils were sent to their knees. They needed all the strength they could get for what the future held.

Neelan and the other missing Anunnaki were still out there.

Are we really just going to sit here? Zara asked aloud, echoing his own thoughts. He knew she didn't mean here, by the stream. He had told them of his conversation with Savar, about how they weren't planning on sending anyone to retrieve the missing people and about how they already knew about SPE. The others had been just as shocked and bitter as he was. He had watched that bitterness fester inside of them just as it had started to in him. He didn't blame them.

What could we even do about it? Ovi asked, still watching Binita out of the corner of his eye, checking on her just to make sure she was okay. *They took the papers we had on SPE.*

As part of their many punishments, they were also not allowed access to cell phones, which almost meant they couldn't use the little internet that Rhapta had.

We should at least be able to do some research, Zara pouted. *I feel useless.*

Kareem agreed, but he didn't know what they could–

I hear they have a stash of smartphones in the Grand Hall, Binita said, cutting off Kareem's thought. They all looked at her. She had stopped throwing stones and turned to face them. *In one of the Advisers' offices,* she added.

They glanced between one another, and Kareem couldn't stop his mind from putting the pieces together, formulating a plan *if* they decided to do such a thing.

It's under lock and key, I assume? Zara asked, but she was smiling.

Of course, Binita said coyly.

Kareem couldn't help his own smile then, and soon, the four of them were grinning at each other.

Are we really going to do this? Ovi asked. *Rescue Neelan and the others on our own? We could get arrested. Or die.* His tone wasn't disagreeable, though.

Kareem glanced at the warrior across the field who had pretended to walk a little closer to them, a silent threat to keep in line, a reminder that they were being watched. Well, Kareem had no intentions of doing what he was told. If Rhapta wouldn't do what was right, he would. And judging by the attentive looks on his team's faces, they would too.

Let's talk about this later, Kareem said, standing. *I'm overdue for a swim.*

DRAMATIS PERSONAE

New Recruits

Kareem Maamoum – Team leader and younger brother to Tejas

Zara al-Hamzi – Kareem's teammate and rival

Ovi Fadel – Kareem's teammate and roommate

Binita Chudasama – Kareem's teammate and Zara's roommate

Caden El Tain – A venari pupil

Idris Lajami – A venari pupil

Faiza Shahd – Friend of Zara and Inaam's roommate

Inaam Kirdar – Friend of Zara and Faiza's roommate

Veer – A venari pupil

Aryan – Younger brother of Waqas

Samira – A venari pupil

Jalla – A venari pupil

Tarun Munir – A venari pupil

Mira – A venari pupil

Kareem's Family

Tejas Maamoum – Kareem's elder brother and venari

Akilah Maamoum – Kareem's young sister

Some of the Venari

    Savar Basu – Head of the Venari

    Zaid Hatem – Apprentice to Savar and the Queen's Consort

    Hessa Darvish – Physical combat instructor

    Amol Khanna – Assistant physical training instructor

    Laban Dayal – Mental conditioning instructor

    Tala – Abilities instructor

    Afif – Human studies instructor

    Neelan Qureshi – Mentor to Keelan's team

    Waqas – A new venari and elder brother of Aryan

    Wael – Friend of Waqas

Ummanu

    Bahati – Watches over the portal in Moshi

    Adam – Watched over the portal in Toronto

GLOSSARY OF TERMS

abilities *(ah bill it ees) n.* Powers that each Anunnaki has. The abilities vary per person and are supernatural in nature.

Anunnaki *(ahn new nock ee) n.* A species thought to have originated from Rhapta to guide humanity. They live longer than humans, can speak to each other telepathically, and have abilities. They reside only in Rhapta. If an Anunnaki leaves the city limits, their abilities fade, and they slowly become human and forget Rhapta. Some live outside the city limits but still within the psychic barrier. Their abilities are weakened, and they have developed a need for verbal speech.

Elder *(ell der) n.* One of the fifty leaders of Rhapta. One out of every fifty is a Grand Elder who leads in ceremony and prophecy.

guakal *(gwa kall) n.* A fist-sized, rigid-shelled, lime-green fruit with miniature red spikes on its exterior; native to Rhapta.

laqueus *(la kwees) n.* A rope, silvery-gray in color, made by Anunnaki used to bind or dampen abilities. Mildly annoying to Anunnaki, physically painful to humans.

magalkan'a *(muh gal kahn uh) n.* Commonly known as Aurastone, believed to be the origin of Anunnaki abilities. Shades range from white to azure.

mark *(mar k) n.* The tribal tattoo that every Anunnaki is born with. Only *venari* and ubir have different tattoos. *Venari's* are larger and need to be reapplied monthly; it allows them to enter the human world while retaining their abilities for a short time. Ubir tattoos are similar but red and swollen, as if infected.

reykalkan'o *(ray kal kon oh) n.* Commonly known as Deathstone. It is cracked Aurastone. Created either by blood magic, or taking it from Rhapta. Its presence is extremely painful to Anunnaki, creating a high-pitched ringing. If the Anunnaki cannot hear it, it's unlikely to be harmful.

Rhapta *(rap tuh) n.* An ancient city located near Mt. Kilimanjaro. It is hidden behind a psychic barrier and unknown to humanity. Currently at half capacity due to its dwindling population.

ubir *(oo beer) n.* Anunnaki that have defected from Rhapta and turned to blood magic to exist outside of the city while retaining their abilities. They quickly become rabid and need to sacrifice humans to retain their abilities. Their Aura is chaotic and painful.

Ummanu *(oo mon oo) n.* Humans who are aware of Anunnaki's existence and have allied with them. Most watch over the portals around the world.

venari *(venn are ee) n.* Anunnaki bounty hunters tasked with locating and returning ubir from human society. They are shunned within Rhapta due to their "dirty" work and closeness with human society.

AUTHOR'S NOTE

Dear Beloved Reader,

Thank you so much for reading *Rise of the Venari*! I'm pleased to introduce the new series, the *Rhaptaverse Chronicles*. This book takes place five years after *The Hidden Prophecy* series, so if you haven't read that yet, I strongly suggest you do. Book 2 is in the works so be on the lookout!

Visit my website (LilySkyy.com) and make sure to sign up for my mailing list to be the first to know about new releases and special happenings such as previews and give-a-ways!

Again, I thank you for reading, and I can't wait to join you on the next adventure!

Sincerely,

Lily Skyy

scan me

Also by Lily Skyy

The Hidden Prophecy Series

Book 1: Cryptic Magic

Book 2: Erratic Magic

Book 3: Infinite Magic

Book 4: Corrupt Magic

The Rhaptaverse Chronicles

(sequel to The Hidden Prophecy)

Prequel Novella: Portal Magic

Book 1: Rise of the Venari

The Unlikely Defenders Series

Book 1: The Unchosen Ones

Book 2: The Unfavorable Heroes

Book 3: The Unlucky Guardians

Book 4: The Unseemly Protectors

Book 5: The Untimely Champions